The plane banked sharply over the island of Singapore. Julie had a sudden intense sense of recognition at the sight of the pale blue water, the winding golden beaches and the line of waving palm trees that fringed the tropical island.

"I'm home," she thought. All at once she felt cold. Her hands were damp where she gripped the armrests, and without knowing when it had happened, she had tears in her eyes. She hadn't realized how much she'd missed Malaya. She had only been a child when war had broken out and she'd been forced to flee with her mother, first from the rubber estate where she'd been born, then from the city of Singapore and finally to England.

She had been five years old. Now she was fifteen. She hadn't seen her father in ten years.

Malaysia, a country of southeast Asia, has been independent since 1963. It is composed of the former Federation of Malaya (where Julie lived before the Japanese invasion) and the former British colonies of Sarawak and British North Borneo (now Sabah). The capital is Kuala Lumpur.

ALL OUR YESTERDAYS

STUART BUCHAN

CROSSWINDS

New York • Toronto
Sydney • Auckland
Manila

First publication August 1987

ISBN 0-373-98006-X

RL 5.7, IL age 11 and up

For my father.

Glossary

amah ....nurse
badju .... tunic
kampong ....native village
sais..chauffeur; driver
sakai........................ native tracker; also a tribe
sampan .... canoelike fishing boat
tanna meara ....red earth; also the name of a town

Chapter One

*A*ll this happened a long time ago.

Chapter Two

The plane banked sharply, coming in at an angle over the island of Singapore, and Julie had a sudden intense sense of recognition at the sight of the pale blue water, the winding golden beaches and the line of waving palm trees that fringed the tropical island.

I'm home, she thought. All at once she was cold. Her hands were damp where she gripped the arm-rests, and without knowing when it had happened, she had tears in her eyes.

She hadn't known how much she missed Malaya. She had been a child when she left here, fleeing with her mother when the war broke out, from the rubber estate where she had been born, first to the city of Singapore, then later to England.

She had been five then. She was fifteen now. She hadn't seen her father in ten years.

The plane leveled, coming in low over the tropical vegetation. She knew if she craned her head she might see the flat roof of the beach house at Tanna Meara where her Aunt Spider lived. Spider had written:

I'll wait until I hear your plane coming in right over the house. Ah Foon and I will stand on the roof with a red sheet in case you can see us. Then I'll get in the car and start for the airport. I'll get there just as you are coming out of customs and immigration.

Julie was startled to see the vivid red sheet there below outlined against the white, white house and then the plane was screaming on, low over the jungle. The wheels came down beneath the plane with a thud that shook the whole plane, and there ahead was the long gray strip of the runway at Changi. They touched down with a bump, bounced once and touched down again.

I'm home, she thought again. The tears had stopped. She felt a great sense of relief. She wanted to get right out of this plane that had taken two days to get her from London to Singapore.

She gathered up her overnight bag and the paperback books she had been reading and moved down the aisle to the door that had been opened. A strong humid wind made her break out in a light perspiration, and then she was at the door of the plane with the steps stretching down onto the runway. She could smell the ripe tropical vegetation and the sea.

In the terminal the immigration officer stamped her passport, smiled at her and said, "Welcome home, Miss Ainsley."

"Thank you."

And she did feel home, she thought, as she gathered her suitcase from the customs officers and moved toward the door.

"Darling!" shouted Aunt Spider, a tiny figure with gray frizzy hair who seemed to just leap out of the crowd and clamp on to Julie. Spider stood back, still holding Julie at arm's length. "My dear, how big you are!" she exclaimed.

And how small you are, Julie thought with wonder. The Aunt Spider she remembered from ten years ago had had black hair, vivid blue eyes and endless energy that made her about the most exciting of Julie's relatives. Julie had lived up on the rubber plantation with her mother and father. Aunt Spider, even ten years ago, had lived down here on the island of Singapore. Coming down to stay a week with Aunt Spider had been one of the things Julie had looked forward most to in her childhood.

Aunt Spider's eyes were still bright blue and as laughing as a child's, but she looked much older and so much smaller to Julie now.

"Oh, I'm so, so glad to see you, darling," Aunt Spider was saying as she signaled for two Malay porters with dark coconut-colored faces and white uniforms to come and take Julie's bag. "I think now the war is finally over."

The war would never be over for Julie. Her mother had died in England. That had happened five years ago when Julie was ten, and for a time she had thought that nothing would ever be able to make her happy again. She hadn't wanted to be happy. She'd thought her heart had maybe literally broken in two. She'd thought that if she were happy, she would be betraying her mother.

And then one day she'd noticed that the apple blossoms were pale pink and white. She'd seen that the spring grass was almost as high as the lowest branches of the trees of the orchard and she knew that although she would always miss her mother, she was going to be happy again sometime. Not right away but sometime.

Aunt Spider had lost none of her energy. She was pushing forward like a life force through the crowd of people. They just stepped out of her way as they saw her tiny figure coming.

"Your father is going to meet your train tomorrow," Aunt Spider said as they came out of the terminal into the eye-searing noon sunshine.

Julie stopped still. She felt the sun on her skin, smelled the sweet perfume of the frangipani blossoms in the still air and let her eyes take in the waving banana palms and the long line of cars with their *sais*, as chauffeurs were called in Malaya, dressed in white uniforms with black velvet hats. She glanced at the rickshaws with their tiny frail carriages and smiled at the three-wheeled bicycles like blown-up children's tricycles with their drivers perched on the seats waiting for customers.

London had been cold and gray and rainy when she'd left. Everywhere she looked here, she saw vivid colors and bright light.

"Come on, come on," Spider was saying as she hurried down the sidewalk to the long black Jaguar limousine. The Malay driver stood grinning at the sight of Julie home.

"Here she is!" Aunt Spider shouted. "Look, isn't she beautiful?"

"Welcome home, Miss Julie," said the old driver whom Spider had employed before the war. He had tears in his eyes.

Julie felt very shy. She didn't know what she had expected of this trip back to Singapore. When her father's letter had arrived, asking her if she would like to come out when the school holidays began, she had at first been afraid, then thrilled and finally nervous. At first she hadn't understood why he hadn't come home to England right after the war to see her. He had been a prisoner of war for four years during the war, as Aunt Spider had, though in different prison camps. And then after the war he had had to go right to the rubber plantation that earned their living to try to get it started again.

Julie had been hurt, but she'd tried to understand. She knew that he must miss her mother almost as much as she did.

Spider pushed her into the car. Her luggage was put in the trunk and then they were drifting down the long driveway to the main road with Spider and Julie in the back and the *sais* in his white uniform and black hat in the front.

"This is the military airport." Spider was chattering on feverishly. "Maybe you remember the other airport at Kalang. That was the civilian airport but it was bombed and now they're repairing it."

What Julie remembered was the bombs falling on the city, the tall plume of smoke from the burning oil depot on the islands out in the harbor, and her mother and herself being raised in a cargo net up the side of the ship that was to take them away from the war.

"Of course, everything will be fixed up one day soon—" Spider was saying. She stopped abruptly to gaze out the window at the gates to the airport. As the car slowed, then turned right onto the road that led out to the beach, Julie saw a *kampong*, a native village, off beyond the low pasture across the road. A bullock was standing in the shade of a banana tree. Two Malay boys in long, bright sarongs, skirts of native cloth that reached their knees, were staring at the big black car.

When they were half a mile farther away from the airport, passing through a small village of wooden stores selling rice and baskets made of woven reeds and Spider still hadn't spoken, Julie said, "I'm glad to be back, Aunt Spider."

Aunt Spider didn't look at her for a long moment.

The car swept on past the village and was traversing a long, yellow dust road through almost deserted fields of banana trees when she turned. "Nothing will ever be exactly the same will it, Julie?" she asked. Her bright eyes were filmed with tears.

"No," Julie admitted. On impulse she leaned over and hugged her frail, courageous aunt.

That was all they said about Julie's mother's death. They both had loved her—after all, she was Aunt Spider's sister—and they would miss her forever, but no words would ever be able to express what they felt.

The yellow dust of the road that rose about the car like a cloud became pink then red, and Julie knew they were approaching the fishing village of Tanna Meara, which means *red earth* in Malay. On her right, she saw the imposing form of Changi prison off across the fields where the prisoners were working. She knew that during the long years of war her aunt had been kept a prisoner there with the other British, and she looked at Spider to see if she was showing the emotions she must have felt to have to pass this prison every day on her way to her home at the beach.

Spider said to her very softly, "I don't let the prison bother me. If I did that, then the past would follow me like a ghost."

"Yes," Julie agreed, but she didn't know if she could have been that brave herself. Sometimes the past crept up on her like an assassin, ambushing her when she least expected it.

Then they were past the prison and its grounds. They drove into the shade of the trees that grew thickly along the sides of the road by the fishing village where the villagers sat crouched like children playing marbles, engaged in their daily routines. Some wove their nets and baskets, others painted the long, low fishing boats while their families cooked on pots over open fires. There was a soothing familiarity to the routine of the fishing village, as though while all the world had been in turmoil, life here had stood still.

At the end of the village, the car gathered speed again, and Julie's heart began to beat more quickly at the thought that soon she would be at the beach house. They slowed, turned through two smashed gateposts and then there ahead, appearing at the end of the long line of frangipani trees whose blossoms filled the car with a heavy perfume, was the sprawling, two-story white house.

The house was exactly as Julie had remembered it.

Memory rushed at her to find her own past here unchanged. She reached out without thinking and took her aunt's small hand in hers and held on tight while the car came out of the shade into the bright sunlight again, made a small circle around the drive and stopped at the steps that led up to the front terrace.

"When I first came here after..." Spider began. Julie knew she meant when she'd first come here after the war ended and she was released with the other prisoners from the camp down the road. "When I first came here," Spider repeated without saying when, "and saw that the house was untouched, it was like a miracle."

"Yes," Julie agreed. "It is a miracle."

"All the furniture and . . . my other things . . . were gone, of course," Spider continued quietly. "But I've learned that things really aren't that important. It's people we must cherish."

They got out of the car and went up the steps to where a beaming Chinese woman in black silk trousers and white tunic was crying and smiling at once.

"Oh, Ah Foon," Julie said, recognizing the old woman who had worked for Aunt Spider all her life. "You're going to make me cry, too."

Then she was hugging Ah Foon and crying, and Spider was clapping her hands loudly so that other servants would come out from the house to take the luggage. There was a rushing all around. Julie and Ah Foon dried their eyes, looking at each other and laughing and crying until Spider said, "You are both going to have to stop that or I'll join in, and I'm getting ugly enough as I get older without weeping all over the place."

Spider, with her frizzed-out gray hair and tiny, tiny face and body had been named Spider long ago by Julie's mother when they were both girls because Spider seemed to be all arms and legs. But she wasn't ugly, no matter what she said about herself. She looked like some comfortable old toy who had been a friend for years and years.

They went into the cool shade of the house, and Julie was drawn silently through one room after another with low rattan furniture and red tiled floors. To the left she saw the dining room with its long table and twelve chairs. Then the light grew much brighter, and she knew that the long living room, which stuck out like a finger pointing on a low peninsula of jungle-hung creepers, was directly ahead.

She might have stepped into one of her own dreams—the dreams that in the long, frightened nights and days of war had kept her heart from dying—for there was the bright blue sea before her and the room with rattan furniture and the green-and-white print of banana leaves on the chair covers. Everywhere she looked were windows almost reaching the floor. She felt as if she were floating in this beautiful room just above the sea.

"You must be hungry," Spider said.

But no, that wasn't what Julie felt. She was suddenly exhausted. The long two-day journey from England and the shock of coming home had overcome her, and she felt as though someone had flung a blanket of sleep over her head.

"Could I lie down, Aunt Spider?" she asked in a small voice.

"Yes, of course, darling," Spider said, understanding immediately.

That was like the old days, too, for Aunt Spider had been one of those wonderful adults who seemed not to have forgotten what it was like to be a child. Because she was so small she sometimes looked almost like a child. Julie had loved her more than anyone except her mother and father.

Ah Foon and Spider took Julie to a cool, shaded room in one wing of the quiet house. Ah Foon fussed around, turning down the bed.

"I really should take a bath first," Julie said weakly.

But they put her onto the bed fully dressed, undid her sandals and covered her with a light cloth. The last sounds she heard before she dropped into what might have been the deepest sleep in years and years, since she left Singapore in fact, was the soft closing of the door, then faintly, faintly at a distance, old sounds that seemed to rise out of the mist of her memory: Malay voices, soft and gentle, speaking somewhere in the garden, the sound of a wild exotic bird crying in outrage then falling silent, and below the house, perhaps truly in her imagination and not loud enough in real life to actually reach her, the lapping of the waves on the red-hot noonday sand of the tropics.

It might have been a dream. She'd had it often since she'd fled the burning city. Or it might have been that when she woke up, she thought she'd dreamed it.

She heard the house servants padding about the room and knew instantly what they were doing. They always got up before dawn's first light broke over the jungle-covered mountains to perform their daily task of rolling up the mats and scrubbing the floor because in the tropics, mold and insects invaded the house unless it was kept spotless.

Julie lay safely in her bed with her bears lined up beside her, each one named and placed in order of rank as she carefully arranged them every night before going to sleep.

As the sun began to climb above the mountains, her old room appeared to her from the shadows. Each

*piece of furniture began to define itself—first the large
closet with her toys, the bureau with her light cotton
sundresses and finally the small table and chairs where
she sometimes had her meals when she was not eating
in the big dining room.*

*Now she began to hear the gardeners arriving to
water the gardens before the hot sun began to blaze.
Snuggling down in her sheets, Julie imagined the
flowering plants: the gardenias, the hibiscus hedges,
the frangipani trees with their fragrant, multicolored
blossoms, refreshed and radiant from their morning
shower.*

*It was time for her father to get up. Julie knew why
he got up so early, earlier than people in America, or
England, or Canada, or anywhere else except where it
was very hot. It was easier to get work done in the cool
early morning or the late afternoon.*

*Julie loved the sound of her father as he went out of
the bedroom at the end of the hall where he slept with
her mother. She followed his footsteps as he pro-
gressed through the house as he went to the front
wicker-lined veranda where he always had his morning tea and breakfast. She listened to the comforting
rumble of his deep voice as he addressed the gardeners and the men from the estate who'd come to him to
plan the day's work.*

*After her father had dismissed the men, Julie
strained her ears to find out whether he was riding or
driving the Jeep. To her delight, he was riding. She
liked the sound of Sultan neighing with his own im-
patience to get his morning exercise.*

When her father had trotted away on Sultan, Julie's amah would come to get her. The amah pulled back the covers and made small chattering talk while she bathed, dressed and took Julie by the hand to lead her to the porch for her own breakfast.

There, sitting on the veranda, Julie could see her whole five-year-old world: the long slope of lawn, the flowering hedges and trees and, farther off, the absolutely straight lines of rubber trees rising like fans into the sunlit sky.

Bounding Julie's world was the jungle draping the slopes of the hills on the far horizons. In it, Julie knew, lived strange and wild creatures: gold-and-black-striped tigers, twenty-foot pythons that slithered along the higher branches of the trees among chattering monkeys and vividly colored birds. And, of course, there were all the jungle flowers and plants, masses of color from the tiniest pale white and green orchids to the blood-red fireplants that splashed the overhanging creepers.

But all that was outside Julie's world. Her world was the self-contained, perfectly ordered estate.

Now she sat eating her breakfast, a boiled egg and toast, fresh juice, a mango or mangosteen. Contentedly she swung her legs, too short to touch the clean, polished wood of the veranda floor, listening for the very best sound of all.

"Hello, darling," her mother said, coming out of the house in her long silk robe. "Come kiss me."

Julie jumped from her chair and was completely enveloped in folds of silk and perfume, by soft lips

and a tight hug—all that Julie remembered of her
mother in the morning.

All this had once been Julie's life. Now as she grew
older in a cold and lonely place, it was her recurring
dream.

When Julie awoke, the long tropical twilight filled
the room. The air was warm and heavy. She felt like a
princess in a fairy story who had just risen from a
spell. She took a bath, changed into a cotton dress and
came out of her room just as the setting sun was making a fire in the sky above the sea. Aunt Spider was
sitting by herself in the long living room, having a cup
of tea.

"This is my favorite time of day," she said, looking up at Julie as she came into the room.

Julie, refreshed as she couldn't remember ever
being—it was like being an entirely new person—went
across the room and sat right on the low stone wall and
looked out over the sea. She could see the dark green
form of the Malay Peninsula go slowly black as eve-
ning came on.

The day seemed to hesitate, unwilling to become
night. Then it folded gradually, the sky becoming first
green, which anywhere else would have astonished the
people but here was so common that no one noticed,
then dark purple and finally black.

Nothing happened for a few long minutes after that,
but Spider didn't speak, knowing what Julie was
waiting for. Then the moon rose like a silver hook
right up out of the dark form of the land across the

sea. The moon hung suspended like a Christmas pantomime set for a while longer, taking its full applause all alone, then slowly one by one the tropical stars that were diamond bright in the black, black sky came out.

Julie sighed.

"There's nothing quite like it, is there?" Spider said softly from the shadowed room behind.

"I was hoping I hadn't just imagined it," Julie murmured, coming away from the wall to sit on a low rattan armchair near her aunt.

"Would you like some tea?" Aunt Spider asked. "I know it's late, but I told cook to hold dinner until you woke up. I'll go tell him he can begin now, but I'm afraid it will be a while yet, anyway."

"Let me go," Julie said, rising.

"Would you? Thank you."

Julie walked through the house that now seemed so wonderfully the same as she had remembered it. She saw that her aunt had had the furniture duplicated to look exactly as it had before the war. She was pleased about that, but still, for one moment, she had an uneasy feeling, as though she had been transported back in time, except she wasn't five years old any longer and she knew what was going to happen.

She shook that thought away. She was fifteen and she had come back to Singapore. The war was over.

In the kitchen the Chinese cook smiled at her, holding up a long kitchen knife as though he might be about to attack the jungle that rose up beyond the window, seen against the night as twisting shadows of vines and very tall trees.

"Ah, missy," he said, beaming.

Julie told him how pleased she was to be home. He told her he was going to prepare her favorite Malaysian chicken. She had forgotten that she had had a favorite chicken dinner, a local dish that was made of chicken and spicy sauces, as well as lemon and some curry. She was almost more surprised to find out that she had forgotten something than to be reminded of how much she had liked that meal. She thought she had remembered every detail of the past.

Aunt Spider had had the lights turned on when she came back to the living room. The room was very bright, and thus the view beyond the room of the dark water and the far-off shore and the sky of stars and moon had faded. Julie was a little sorry, but at the same time she was glad that the room was so brightly lit. It looked happy and cheerful with the green-and-white print.

"Cook says dinner will be one hour," she told her aunt.

"Good. That will give us time for a nice chat."

Julie sat near her aunt again. Neither of them really knew where to begin. Finally her aunt said, "I want to tell you about your father."

Julie was a little frightened but said nothing. She had loved her father very much, so much that he'd seemed almost like a god to her for the first five years of her life. Then in one swift moment he had disappeared for ten long years.

"He's not exactly as he was," Aunt Spider said.

Julie hadn't expected that he would be. She wasn't exactly as she had been, either.

But then Spider, reading Julie's mind as she always had, said, "I don't mean that he was wounded or anything. He's quieter. That's what I mean. He doesn't talk about his experiences in camp. Lots of people don't. They just want to forget them and go on. It's healthier, though of course very difficult."

"I'm just so pleased that I'm going to see him," Julie said tremulously.

"Oh, my dear," Spider said, folding her tiny monkeylike hands. "I know what you must have thought. You must have thought that he loved you less because he didn't come to find you right away."

Once she had. But then she had made herself stop thinking that. "No," Julie said, not able to look at her aunt because part of what she was about to say was a lie. "I didn't think he didn't love me. But . . ."

"But what darling?" Aunt Spider asked so quietly that she might not even have spoken.

Julie looked at her aunt, and she couldn't help it: there were tears in her eyes. "But I thought he would know that I missed him," she said.

She started to cry, very different tears than the tears she had shed earlier on arrival. Those had been tears of sentiment. These were tears from her heart, months and months, years and years of loss coming right out now that she was here among her family again.

Spider rose slightly, but Julie just flew from where she sat right into her aunt's arms and they hugged each other. Julie cried for a while, but not as long as you might think. After her long dream, some of the past seemed to have been washed away. When she stopped she just stopped dead, the tears drying up with a deep sob.

Spider took a lace handkerchief embroidered in the rough-colored embroidery of the natives and wiped her niece's eyes.

"I just want to see him," Julie said.

"And he's waiting for you," Spider told her. "When he came out of the camp he learned about Betty's death, and I think that something cracked for him right then, if you understand me."

Betty had been Julie's mother, now dead.

"I mean," Spider said, "he had been in camp and I think he expected perhaps to die because we all did, but we didn't expect either of you to die. We thought you were *safe*," she said, and Julie heard the anger in Spider's voice.

"It didn't seem *right*!" Spider added more quietly. "It didn't seem fair, though of course one learns not to expect things to be fair. Not always." She hugged Julie hard again and then sat back. "Now," she said. "I want you to tell me as much as you think you can bear about the years we've not seen each other. We have to sometime, and when we have talked about it, we don't have to do so again."

So Julie told her about what she remembered of the long journey by ship, traveling at night with the lights out to avoid the submarines, of arriving first in India and then, later, flying on to England. She told her about the bombs falling on London at night, of how they had huddled in the subway stations, sleeping on beds that had been set out, of the way the bombs had sounded, of how when they'd come out in the morning they never knew if the house where they lived would still be standing or whether it would be part of the piles of smoking rubble. She told her aunt how her mother had found a centuries-old house in the country that was very, very beautiful, with beamed ceilings inside and unkempt but large gardens outside. They'd lived there with another woman and her child, a boy, who'd fled the bombs of London, too. The house had no electricity because it had been built in the sixteenth century. At night they'd all gone to bed with candles. Because of wartime rationing, they'd had to exist on very little food.

When the worst moment had come and Julie had to tell her aunt of how her mother had died, not from bombs or war, but from a heart that just seemed to give out on her one day, Julie had to stop.

"You don't have to go on, dear," Spider said.

But after a moment, as the little bugs flew around the lights of the house in Singapore, so far, far away from that large dark house in England, Julie was able to tell her aunt that, also.

Then she went on to tell about the cousins who had taken her in, the boarding school and the long wait for her father to come for her.

During all this, Spider listened intently, her eyes enormous in her tiny face. Sometimes she made Julie stop, provide a detail or go back to repeat something as though because they had agreed to talk about it once and never discuss it again, she had to memorize it all.

After Julie was finished, there was a long silence. They heard the sounds of the kitchen through the house. They heard the water below the house. Finally Julie stood up and walked back to where she had been sitting on the low window ledge. She saw that now the fishing boats—light boats almost like large canoes—had left the shore, trailing the lights.

Behind her, Spider sighed. Julie turned. "Yes," she said. "It was a terrible time."

"You young people..." her aunt began, then stopped.

The house servant came in and announced dinner was served right at that moment, and whatever Spider might have been going to say about the young was lost in the move from one room to the next.

The dining room was perfect, with flowers that Julie hadn't seen in years on the table: white gardenias like the soft cheeks of young girls, floating in low green jade bowls. There were candles here, too, low ones that floated in other clear crystal bowls like fallen stars.

Partway through dinner, her aunt asked, "Do you remember Douglas Diamond?"

"No."

"He lived on the next estate at Bukit Timor," she said, naming another rubber town in the northern peninsula close to where Julie had grown up.

"I don't remember him."

"No, you wouldn't, I suppose," her aunt said. What she meant was that the estates were so big that for one child—or, for that matter, an adult—to visit another in the country required enormous preparations. They had to make telephone calls and arrange cars and drivers and it wasn't worth going just for an afternoon, so usually they went overnight. So naturally most people in the country just lived by themselves and seldom saw their neighbors.

"He's about a year older than you are," her aunt said. "But he wasn't as lucky as you were. He was caught here with his family, and he spent the whole war in prison camp."

Julie tried to think of what it would be like to be sent to a prison camp at six and stay there for four years. She had been about to protest that she had had a terrible time in the war. Her mother had died. But she kept quiet.

"He should have gone back to England to boarding school after the war." Spider was saying each word very carefully as though she wanted Julie to listen to each one and remember it. "But his family didn't think it was right to send him right away after that terrible experience, so he stayed." She gave a very small shrug and went on, "His father's estate was destroyed in the war, and he now works for your father."

Spider sighed and stopped talking while the dishes were cleared and dessert was passed. Julie recognized the wonderful mangosteen fruit that she hadn't tasted in ten years.

When the servants were gone again, Spider continued. "He's going to travel up country with you tomorrow on the train, I think. So you should look for him on the train."

"All right," Julie agreed.

"Doug was in the camp that we passed down the road."

"With you," Julie said.

"Yes." Another pause, then, "He comes back to it sometimes. He can't seem to forget it."

They left the dining room and went into the living room again. Now it was Aunt Spider who was tired. After a short time talking about unimportant things, she rose and kissed Julie. "I am so, so happy to have you back," she said.

When Spider had gone to bed, Julie, who after her long sleep, wasn't tired at all, watched the play of the fishing fleet. They had gathered almost exactly halfway between the two shores, a small village of boats with their lights sparkling on the water.

Her aunt came into the room behind her again, dressed now in a light robe. "Be careful if you leave the house," she said. "The gardener killed a cobra on the front terrace last week. He had wrapped himself around the water pipe. They always travel in twos, you know. So his mate will perhaps come looking for him."

Then before she left the room, she said almost to herself, "Isn't it curious that even snakes seem to need another creature all their own?"

Julie shivered. She had forgotten some of the small rules and cautions that you had to take in the tropics.

The moon seemed to have grown larger as it had risen above the dark water. Julie felt restless. After a few minutes of indecision, she decided that if she were careful she could go into the narrow strip of garden to the side where the steps had led down to the beach.

She walked back through the almost silent house and out onto the front terrace, making a wide sweep around the water pipes that were used by the gardener. The snakes would have gone to that spot for the water, which they took in through their skin. On the estate after a heavy tropical rain you had to be careful where you walked on the long sweep of lawn that sloped away from the house because they would lie out there in the wet. They were harmless unless you frightened them.

But then, Julie thought, as she walked through the garden smelling the night-blooming flowers, most people were dangerous, too, when they were frightened.

Out in the garden, the night was indeed much darker, the deep, velvet darkness of countries near the equator. Julie stood with her arms crossed over her chest, not thinking anything for quite a while, but just looking at the liquid sky and the stars. She watched the fishing fleet as it moved across the water and saw how one small sampan—for that is what the Malay fishing boat is called—had moved off to one side of the fleet all by itself.

Soon she found she was thinking of her mother. So much had happened in the past years—almost all Julie's life—that she had learned not to be as upset the way a child, or young girl, who had grown up in a regular place at a regular time might have been. She thought tonight of how all through the war her mother had kept alive the memory of Julie's father by always talking about him at night before Julie went to bed. They would sit by his picture and sometimes Julie saw her mother cry.

To Julie, he was still the man in the picture. A young man standing by his horse in his riding clothes, rubber trees and a corner of the house behind him. She remembered Spider saying he had changed. Would he still love her? She hoped so. She hoped that she would love him, too, love him the way her mother had loved him. Then she began to wonder if she would ever love anyone that passionately herself.

The small sampan that had detached itself from the fishing fleet was moving like a tiny night beetle trailing its long tail of light across the water toward the near shore. Julie wondered if the fisherman had his catch already and was on the way home.

He came in to the shore, then turned almost directly to the part of beach under the garden where she stood. This was a private beach and no one was ever meant to land there. You couldn't reach it in any way except by sea.

Julie thought of calling for someone from the house, but then she thought that that would be silly. He was probably just one of the fishermen who had

had some trouble with his nets and now he needed to make for the closest shore to repair it so he could go back to the fleets to get his night's catch.

As the sampan passed close into land, it vanished from Julie's sight. She relaxed, looking out at all this quiet beauty, glad to be back.

It must have been some minutes later that she heard it. At first it was a soft moving nearby, and of course she thought immediately of the cobra. She stood frozen with fear, listening to leaves rustling. She restrained a cry because she would look a fool for being out here when she had been told to watch out for the snake.

Something was approaching. Now she was terrified, and she tried to calm herself by reminding herself that only when the snake was scared would it rise up, spread its fan and strike. If it did that, she would die. Cobras are killers. She didn't know if she could stand absolutely still as she would have to if it came out of the jungle vines that fell away down the sides of the steps that led to the beach.

At first she wasn't sure they were footsteps. They were soft, surreptitious, and while the thoughts of the snake approaching faded, other thoughts of a thief creeping up from the beach where he must have landed on his sampan started her heart beating faster.

She could feel her throat opening again and knew that she could scream, but just before she did he seemed to erupt right out of the night before her, passing up the cliff face and over the last step as though he had exploded out of the darkness.

Then he was no more than a foot from her, eyes bright in the moonlight, face darkly tanned. She couldn't tell what he was wearing, but she knew instantly that, though he was tanned as dark as a Malay, he was English like herself.

They stood looking at each other, both frightened before a flash of anger transformed his handsome face. He stepped forward and pushed her quite deliberately out of his way and ran off toward the gates to the grounds.

Julie recovered. She should, she thought, tell someone. She wasn't scared anymore. She thought she knew who he was. He had to be the boy who had spent the war years in the prison camp down the red dust road with his family and Aunt Spider, the boy who Spider said kept coming back to the camp, *Douglas Diamond*.

Chapter Three

In the frenzy of leaving the house early in the morning to catch the North Star Express to Kuala Lumpur where her father would meet her, Julie didn't mention the strange wild-eyed boy who had come up from the beach the night before.

Spider was saying, "Oh, how I wish you could stay a day or two more before you go home to the estate, but your father is so anxious to see you."

Julie's thoughts were with the man up country who would be meeting her train. He had waited five years to summon her home.

"I'll come down in a few weeks, Aunt Spider," she said.

"Yes, of course you will," Spider said, bustling her toward the front terrace.

The servants were lined up to say goodbye just as though she had been here for a long stay. They used to do that in the old days, and she was touched as she said goodbye to each of them. At the very end she accepted the small red-paper-wrapped package from Ah Foon. She knew red paper stands for good luck to the Chinese.

Spider and Julie drove away through the early morning light, as bright as searchlights, passing the prison that seemed to float like an enormous castle across the fields. Rows of prisoners were out hoeing the ground behind the wire fences. Some of them looked up curiously as the long black car passed, trailing clouds of red dust from the dry roadbed.

Spider was chattering on about the changes that Julie would see as they got closer to town, but Julie's mind had drifted away to the boy with the angry eyes. She thought of speaking to Spider about him, but she knew she would have to explain why she had disobeyed her aunt's admonition to go around the garden and she thought also that she might get the boy in trouble.

She wasn't at all sure he was Douglas Diamond now. She realized what a leap of coincidence she had made in her mind when she'd decided that. The moon floating above the water and the smell of the flowers had brought an emotional mood to her homecoming. She had wanted everything to be absolutely neat and tied up. To have Douglas come up the steps from the beach would have seemed right.

She couldn't remember now exactly what Douglas had been like as a child. She tried to recall him, but she had been very young then and much had happened since she'd left here. She had a vague memory of a dark-haired boy who had no fear of anything, who was always being called back from going too deep into the water where sharks lurked or trying to ride his pony too fast or playing near the jungle.

She thought again of speaking to her aunt about him, but just then Spider said, "There."

Beyond the window was Singapore Harbor, the last sight that Julie had seen as a child the day she and her mother had fled the bombed city. The harbor today looked so placid that Julie was almost angry. The day they had left, a pall of yellow dust had risen from the bombed buildings. The Chinese section of the city had been in flames because many of their low two-story buildings were made of wood. All along the waterfront had risen the whine, like an enormous insect, of car engines being left to grind themselves dry so the Japanese, who would soon take over the city, couldn't use them.

Now, where the last plume of black smoke had risen from the burning oil reserves on the islands out in the harbor, there were green knolls on a sunlit sea. Sampans ran between the large liners. The war had come and gone and left no mark out in the harbor.

The long wharfs at Kepple Harbor thrusting out into the water looked exactly as they had in her memory, except there were fewer people. That day years ago, thousands of people had pushed toward the launches going out to the last ships waiting to run from the approaching war. Now she saw porters and taxi drivers, customs inspectors and all types of vendors selling everything from noodles to little pink plastic dolls and big bright kites.

Can this be true? she was wondering as her outrage died down. Could a war go through a country and leave so little mark?

Then they were beyond the harbor and Spider was pointing out where buildings she thought Julie might remember had disappeared entirely from the city.

"That was Woo's Chinese department store. Do you remember?" Spider was saying as she pointed to an empty space among the buildings. All Julie saw was an open area already thickly covered with trees and vines.

The way Spider suddenly stopped speaking, however, told Julie that though to her the city looked the same, it didn't to her aunt. Every vacant lot was to Spider a reminder of all that had happened.

Her aunt was making an effort not to cry. "That was J. B. David's house," she said, pointing to a mansion on the low hill that rose up almost in the center of the city. "He was the Chinese rice millionaire. They used his house to torture people."

Julie put her hand over Spider's. All thoughts of talking about the boy coming up from the beach vanished. After all, her aunt would be quite safe in her house. She was surrounded by servants to look after her and the boy, though he had looked very angry when he'd seen Julie, hadn't looked dangerous.

He'd looked shocked, she decided. That's how he had looked. Shocked to see her. He had probably been coming in from the water at night for a good while. What harm could that do? People shouldn't have private beaches, anyway.

They were passing now through an older section of the city where the imposing Episcopalian cathedral faced out over a long green park. Julie recognized more buildings, though not clearly, and then they were coming toward the railroad station and Spider erupted into a burst of activity. She told the *sais* where to park the car, called for porters almost before they had slowed, and was out supervising Julie's two simple suitcases as soon as the car had drawn to a stop.

They followed the porters into a station that was like a bazaar: the first-class passengers all gathered to one side in their white suits and print dresses, the second-class passengers, mostly Chinese and Malay, flowing like water all about the station, with their luggage that was made up of old suitcases, parcels tied with string, open cages of chickens and ducks and bags of strange herbs bought in the Chinese part of town so they could make their own spices.

Julie looked at her own two shabby suitcases that her cousin had pulled from the attic in England.

"I should probably be riding second class," she murmured to her aunt as she looked at the stiff first-class passengers who looked very conscious of their position.

"Oh, my dear," Spider said, bustling as though it was up to her to get all these people on the train to

Kuala Lumpur. "Luggage means nothing. It's character that counts."

Julie was so startled by her aunt's words that she burst into laughter.

Spider looked at her. "Am I being ridiculous?" she asked. "Yes, I suppose I am. But after you've spent four years in a prison for no reason at all except that you have white skin, you see everything differently. We're all the same. You know that, don't you?"

She seemed to have to make this point, for she leaned forward and took hold of Julie's arm again with her tiny monkey hand. "If anything good at all is to come out of that terrible war, it has to be that. We have to forget our ridiculous pretension of class and money and skin color and admit we're all part of one large family."

Julie wasn't prepared for this sudden sermon. She stammered, "Yes, yes," and saw how the first-class passengers who had heard most of this and understood quite well that it was directed against them drew together in a group. She could tell that they were going to look at her with suspicion on the journey, but she was proud of her tiny, birdlike aunt and said very loudly, "Yes Aunt, I agree with you."

Spider was shocked by Julie's intensity. She stood back, blinked once or twice quickly like a furious parrot interrupted in speech and said very quietly, "Good."

Julie, dressed in her beige cotton traveling dress, felt pale compared to the dusky skins of the people who had grown up here. I would have looked like that, she thought, noticing a girl, older than herself, who stood reading a magazine as though she were entirely alone on the platform. The girl had long sun-streaked blond hair and skin like coffee with a lot of cream in it. The heat, which now was creeping up into the nineties though it was still early morning, didn't faze the girl. She might have been reading her magazine in front of a fan for all the discomfort she showed.

Aunt Spider was saying, "Where is he?"

"Who?"

"Douglas," Spider said. She looked at Julie and said impatiently, "I told you last night. There!" she pointed at a figure who had appeared in the door to the station.

The light was behind him and Julie might have got a good look at him, but the train conductors behind her suddenly threw open the gates to the track and the crowd surged forward.

"Oh, he is so irritating!" Spider said, grabbing Julie's hand. "One knows of course that he's had a terrible, terrible time but somehow one must *cope*." She grabbed a porter with her free hand, and the next thing Julie knew she was part of the multiracial, multicolored crowd flowing through the gates toward the stately railroad carriages that waited to take them to the north of the country.

The train astonished her. It might have been preserved in some very safe place all through the war, for it was made up of pristine clean red-and-gold carriages, some with a big gold crest of the railroad line emblazoned on them.

She could remember this train vividly now that it stood before her again, taller than the newer trains that were now beginning to appear on English railroad lines. The engine, which she could see now that Spider was pushing purposefully forward, gleamed like some ancient mythical beast, jet black and spotlessly clean.

"It's the same train!" she exclaimed.

"Yes," Spider agreed, finding the carriage she was looking for.

The porter climbed in ahead of them to stow Julie's bags and then returned for the tip.

By this time the platform was almost empty. Julie was afraid she would miss her train. "Douglas!" Spider shouted. Julie jumped. She turned to find herself almost face-to-face with the boy from the night before.

She moved back quickly, startled by the intensity of his blue gaze. His face, deeply tanned, as she observed it in the better light of the station, seemed much more mature than the face of any sixteen-year-old boy she had met in England.

"Douglas," said Spider in a voice that was calm again. "I thought you would miss the train."

"No, Spider," he said. "I won't miss the train."

Julie was surprised to hear him call her aunt *Spider*. But then of course they had spent years together behind those barbed-wire fences and he did appear older than his years. He stood almost to his full growth, six feet or so, and though he was gaunt he looked very strong, as though he'd already had a life of hard work behind him.

He looked now at Julie with a curiously disturbing look, very calm, assessing her quite openly as though he was deciding whether he wanted to be friends. "You're Julie," he stated.

Julie felt awkward and young. She knew to her mortification that she would blush any moment and that with her white, untanned skin used to the pale light of England, it would be very obvious how embarrassed she was.

Sure enough, the blush began. Douglas Diamond watched for a few seconds as Julie felt her face begin to color. She thought that the ice-blue eyes in the dark face began to smile, though the lips, which were very full, didn't. Finally, to her relief, he turned to Spider and said, "I'll deliver her, Spider," just exactly as though he were talking about a mule or a sack of onions.

Julie might have protested in spite of her embarrassment. She was quite capable of getting from Singapore to Kuala Lumpur on a train, thank you. At five years old with her mother, she had fled a burning city and made it easily to England. She could cover eight hundred miles in a red-and-gold first-class carriage without getting lost.

But right then there was a piercing whistle that demanded they board the train. The conductors from within started to shout. From up and down the platform, other officials began in unison to wave red flags.

Chapter Four

The train moved forward three or four feet, then stopped. Spider grabbed Julie and hugged her, then jumped away as the train whistle shrieked again impatiently. Julie felt arms lift her from beneath her elbows as the train began to gather speed.

Her feet touched the deck of the train and a laughing conductor pulled her on board. The hands holding her arms released her, and she turned to see Douglas Diamond running alongside the moving train.

He threw his bag on the platform at Julie's feet, reached out and swung up. For a second he was suspended and Julie's heart rose into her throat. He would fall beneath the fast-moving steel wheels, she was sure of it, but she had been right about how strong he was. As the train moved out into the light from the cool of the station, he swung himself effortlessly on board.

"We're off," he said to her with that same flat, calm voice.

They turned to wave together to Spider, but the opening to the station where the rails went in was now a gray, dim spot in a fiercely lighted landscape, and she was lost to their sight.

Julie went to find her seat. The porters had put her luggage very nicely into a rack in a first-class carriage. The Englishman and his wife looked at her with a smile as she came in.

"Hello," the woman said. "Your first time in Malaya?"

"No," said Julie. "I was born here."

"*Were* you, my dear?" the woman asked in surprise.

"Yes," Julie told her, taking her seat across from them on the plush velvet bench. "But this is my first time back since I was a child." She saw Douglas pass outside in the corridor and wished he would come in, but he cast one look at her companions and went on down the corridor.

"That must have been a few years ago," said the man, leaning forward solicitously. Julie realized that to everyone out here now everything related to the war. Now that she had told them she had been born here and had been away, they knew she had left when the war had come and now was returning.

She felt tired suddenly, though she had only been up and around for a few hours. She didn't want to have to go into the long story of what had happened to her during the war and why she was back.

"Yes," she said curtly in what might have been taken as rudeness. She turned to look out the window at the gardens of the houses they were passing as the train fled toward the sea. The gardens were very large and filled with an astonishing variety of flowers. English gardens were much shyer in their beauty, she decided.

The door opened and a very fat Chinese man came in, looking furious. "Is this my seat?" he demanded, pointing to an empty seat.

"I don't know, sir," said the Englishman in a voice that implied he thought it rude to be asked because after all he wasn't the conductor.

"I think this is my seat," the Chinese man insisted. He filled the whole door of the carriage so Julie only had a glimpse of Douglas Diamond as he came back and went past in the corridor.

"Have you checked your ticket?" the Englishman asked.

"It *is* my seat," the Chinese gentleman announced, without looking at his ticket. He turned sideways and got his enormous bulk into the carriage. When he sat down at the other side of the bench from Julie, she felt it move up as though he had got on the other end of a seesaw. She almost giggled, then stifled her laugh by looking at the Englishwoman. But the Englishwoman was almost laughing, too, making a big show of putting her handkerchief to her mouth to cough to cover her laughter.

"These trains are not like they used to be," the Chinese man said to the Englishman. "They used to be more comfortable."

"Are you sure?" the Englishman asked him in what might have passed for genuine interest, except that his face was completely devoid of expression. "They seem about the same to me."

"Not at all," the Chinese man said with satisfaction. "Nothing is the same since the war."

That, Julie thought, seemed to be the theme of everything in Malaya these days. She began to think idly about her father. She was still nervous about seeing him, but now that the second part of her journey had begun, the journey into the interior of the country, she felt more relaxed, soothed by the steady clicking of the wheels on the rails.

"We'll be coming to the causeway soon," the Englishwoman said to Julie.

"Of course if we had blown up the causeway properly," the Englishman was saying to his wife, "the enemy troops couldn't have crossed into the city so fast. All we did was blow up about six feet in the middle. Idiots."

"But if we had done that," the Chinese gentleman said, sounding shocked, "we wouldn't be riding across on the causeway today. It might have taken years to repair!"

"It did," the Englishman said shortly, referring to the four years of war when the causeway had been in the hands of the enemy.

Julie felt she had to get out of this carriage. She felt trapped with characters out of some adult film she didn't understand. She got up, saying, "Excuse me," to the Chinese gentleman as she stepped over his plump legs, which stuck straight out like high hurdles.

She felt better as soon as she was in the corridor. Where could Douglas Diamond be? She wanted to thank him for helping her get on the train. Without his help she might have been standing right now beside Aunt Spider, looking at an empty track. She would have felt like an absolute fool if she had missed her train to meet her father.

The corridor was empty. She started to move toward the next carriage but when she opened the door at the end, she saw that between each carriage there was a little bridge, longer and more stable than the connection on an English train, with a small railing along the side and a floor beneath so passengers could stand. A sign just inside the door told you to do no such thing but that was where Douglas Diamond stood. He was on the bridge watching the causeway draw closer with the speeding train.

"Hello," Julie said.

The look the bright eyes gave her wasn't friendly. "Hello." He turned back to watching the water.

Julie, somewhat scared, stood near him. The train clattered onto the first rungs of the causeway with a hollow sound and then they were passing over, away from the island of Singapore and heading toward the distant shore of the Malayan peninsula. The water was a long, long way below, and watching it, Julie felt herself getting dizzy.

She hadn't known that she was wobbling until he put his arms about her and helped her back into the train. "That was very stupid," he told her in the same expressionless voice he had used earlier. He acted as though his body was here on the train heading north but his mind was elsewhere.

"I was looking for you!" she said.

She thought he would at least ask why, but he didn't. He stood watching her as though he had come on a particularly strange type of creature, a jungle monkey, perhaps, that he had never seen before.

"I wanted to thank you for helping me onto the train."

"That's all right," he said finally. He still hadn't taken his eyes off her face, and she was feeling very young, very strange and suddenly irritable.

"You could fall off out there," she told him in what she knew was a bossy voice.

The way he stared at her without answering for a long moment made her think that he was quite properly going to say it was none of her business, and then naturally she would counter with some remark about how she felt close to him because they had been friends as children and then they would have a real conversation. Perhaps they would sit down and have a soft drink together.

Instead he said seriously, "I don't like to be inside places," and turned around and went back through the door to the outside bridge between the carriages.

Julie returned to her seat. The two English people and the very fat Chinese man were sitting in silence. She watched from her window seat as the jungle seemed to flow down toward the train tracks, passing on both sides, broken sometimes by a small *kampong* made of thatched-roof huts that sat high off the ground on stilts to provide air and keep wild beasts out.

Before she knew it, it was time for lunch. "Would you like to join us, dear?" the Englishwoman asked her.

Julie looked toward the door to the carriage, hoping that Douglas Diamond would turn up, but all she saw were other diners passing on their way to the dining car. "Yes, please," she said. She had felt very much at home the day before, but now she felt like a stranger again.

They went down the length of the train to a very clean dining car where stewards in white uniforms were waiting. Each table of four seats had a lace tablecloth and blue-and-white tableware. The knives and forks and spoons seemed to be silver and they had a crest of the railway on them.

"This is new," the Englishman said, picking up the silver appreciatively.

His wife introduced herself as Mrs. Wentworth. Mr. Wentworth was retired. They had lived on an estate themselves most of their lives, and they, too, had fled the country at the beginning of the war. But they had spent the war in India. "Very hot," Mrs. Wentworth

said, touching her throat with a delicate handkerchief.

"No hotter than here before the monsoon rains,"
her husband insisted.

"Perhaps India just seems hotter." Mrs. Wentworth retreated.

"Because it's dirtier," her husband said emphati-
cally. "Malaya is clean."

"Yes," his wife said vaguely, looking out at the
slopes of unbroken jungle as though inspecting it for
dust.

The fourth seat that Julie was hoping to save for
Douglas was taken by a nice, timid woman who
seemed to have mixed blood—part European and part
Malayan. She was astonishingly beautiful with big luminous eyes and long silky hair that flowed from an
absolutely perfect parting in the center of her head,
down beside her face like a frame. Julie, who could
hardly take her eyes off her, felt more and more plain.
The woman said she was a teacher in Kuala Lumpur.
Then she concentrated on the meal that came with
perfect service, course after course.

The Wentworths carried on a long, desultory conversation with each other about India versus Malaya.
Julie was sure they had had this conversation a
hundred or more times but they circled the subject like
vultures, pouncing on each new detail, each insight,
each piece of evidence to show that they had chosen
the better country to retire in.

Julie saw the teacher looking at the Wentworths
from time to time with sly amused little glances from

under wonderful long eyelashes. She thought the Wentworths were a huge joke, Julie could see, and once when she caught Julie's eye by mistake, she winked.

Julie loved her. In a second she had made Julie feel at home again in a way that the Wentworths, though they were English, never could have.

"Ah," said Mr. Wentworth pushing back from the table finally. "That was a good tiffin."

"Very adequate," said his wife primly.

Julie, who had spent the war years in England where everything was rationed—you got a tiny piece of meat each week, one egg and few treats like the dessert that they had just had of lichee nuts swimming in syrup— looked astonished. A family could have lived for a week in England during the war on what Mr. and Mrs. Wentworth had put away in an hour. She thought that they were very lucky to have ended up in India with all its shortcomings from their point of view. They would have been very unhappy in England.

They asked her if she was ready to leave the table. She said she would stay a few minutes more to look at the view that was now one of long sloping valleys and distant peaks all shining in the noonday sun. What she was hoping was that the teacher would stay and she did, looking away while the Wentworths lumbered to their feet and went off down the carriage.

"Not everyone is like that," she said to Julie, apologizing but also watching them fondly as they tried to get themselves across the little bridge outside the carriage. "They're dodos but they don't know it yet."

She told Julie that she taught in a large school in Kuala Lumpur. She was half English ("Scottish really. My father was a sailor.") and half Malay. She had never seen England and was curious for every detail Julie could supply. Julie, who thought England was a very poor second to this wonderful country passing beyond the windows, did her best to supply what details she could but she felt sadly inadequate to the task.

She had lived in England a long time, but she had never felt it to be her home, so she hadn't really tried to memorize anything in the way she had memorized every detail of her early life on the rubber plantation.

Still, the young teacher seemed satisfied. "I should love to travel to England someday," she said wistfully, putting her chin in her hand while she watched the view.

"It's not nearly as nice as this," Julie told her.

"Oh, it must be!" the young woman insisted.

"It's much colder."

"I should like that."

When they had parted, Julie went back to her seat, thinking how curious it was that almost everyone wanted to be somewhere else. She wanted to be here. The young teacher wanted to be in England. Perhaps the Wentworths weren't so strange, after all: they had chosen the country where they wanted to live out their lives and were sticking to their decision.

She had forgotten Douglas in the excitement of the enormous lunch and the discussion with the lovely young woman. Now she wondered when he was going to have his lunch. With the second sitting, she decided, as the dining car could only accommodate half the first-class passengers at one time. But perhaps because he didn't like to be inside anywhere, he didn't want to go in for lunch and he'd be hungry.

She was back at her seat before she saw him. The carriage seemed to have been put under a spell in her absence. Everyone was asleep. The Chinese gentleman was sprawled over most of the bench where Julie had been sitting, and both the Wentworths had dropped into a deep slumber. Mr. Wentworth slept straight up, as though he were on guard, but Mrs. Wentworth had somehow flowed across the seat as though the heat had melted her. Her mouth opened and closed and she snored in the most ladylike way, little rumbles coming from her well-bred nose as though she thoroughly disapproved of everything she was dreaming.

Julie squeezed across all of them to her seat without waking them. She thought adults very strange the way they could sleep in public. Sleeping in public was somewhat like bathing in public, absolutely unthinkable unless you were in a bomb shelter.

The heat in the carriage played its magic on Julie herself, however, and she closed her eyes to rest them from the very bright light reflected off the unbroken field of green beyond the window.

Within a fraction of a second, she was asleep.

Chapter Five

The dream came at her out of the past, rising from a dark mist that at first she thought was the burning plume of smoke above the oil depots in the harbor, but then she saw that it was the night, the deep, deep night.

"Come on, darling, wake up very quietly," she heard her mother's gentle voice say.

Her mother was crouched by her bed. She had pushed the mosquito net back, so she seemed to have a cloud of white behind her head, a cloud that rose all the way to the dark ceiling far above Julie's five-year-old head.

Julie stretched, uncertain why her mother had come to wake her. Her amah usually came to wake her, but later, when the household was already awake and it was daylight.

"You must get up now, Julie," her mother said.

Julie struggled out of the bed where her mother had flung back the covers. Still half asleep, she stood while she went through the unfamiliar ritual of having her mother dress her in the dark.

Then they were walking through the dark, silent house. She could hear the servants in some distant place, but everyone was moving very quietly, and when they came out on the long veranda in the front there was the car with her father sitting behind the wheel where the sais *usually sat.*

"Hurry, Betty," he called, keeping his voice low, and then they were all three of them, mother, father and daughter, in the front seat. Julie until that time had never ridden in the front seat of the car. The sais *drove and perhaps one of the servants rode up front with him, sometimes even one of the men from the estate, but never Julie or her mother.*

Her father had the headlights off, and the car coasted down the long road out of the estate, past the ghostly rubber trees planted in symmetrical rows for as far as the eye could see.

When they came to the main road, there were many other cars heading in the same direction, south, and they joined them. They had their headlights on for a while. A few army lorries filled with troops flew past them in the other direction.

Then with a terrible noise, as though someone had torn a hole in the skin of the sky and the world itself

*was screaming, planes came down out of the night,
low above the convoy of cars and trucks. The bullets
struck in every direction. Julie's mother pulled her low
onto the seat.*

*It seemed to Julie the longest night that she'd ever
passed.*

*Dawn came up over the jungle-swathed mountains
as they entered the small village of Bukit Timor. Here
they could see one of the tributaries of the larger river.
The river was filled with boats of every description:
large launches from the estates and oil companies,
yachts that looked as if they were on an afternoon
cruise, native boats, sampans and some fishing boats
caught upriver. All the people in them were as silent as
though turned to stone as the boats floated down-
river.*

*They went through Bukit Timor and headed south
again and the day got very hot. They stopped, but all
they could get was water. Julie's mother was worried
that it hadn't been boiled to keep the germs out. All
other food seemed to have vanished from every shop.*

*Julie was sick and frightened. She clung to her
mother. Her mother and father said nothing as they
drove on. One plane came back and she could feel her
mother tense. The rows of cars and trucks kept moving, but the plane just circled slowly as though it had
all the time in the world and disappeared back over the
mountain range.*

*After a long time, they came to the outskirts of Ku-
ala Lumpur. The small Moslem city was awash with
noise and panic. People ran in every direction. Her*

*father's handsome face was gray and drained as he
headed for the tall onion-shaped domes of the railroad station.*

*The station was under military rule. Soldiers
stopped people who tried to force their way toward the
trains. But they let Julie and her mother through. It
wasn't until her mother turned to hug her father for a
long half minute, clinging to him so she almost
squeezed Julie's breath out of her as she was held between them, that Julie understood her father was
staying behind.*

*"I love you, Betty" were his last words to Julie's
mother, then to Julie, "Look after Mummy. Will you
promise?"*

"Yes, Daddy."

*He kissed her, holding her close, then he released
her and the crowd pushed them forward toward the
last train.*

*"Daddy!" Julie cried, "Daddy! Come with us!
Don't leave us!"*

*But he was lost to her sight. Night was coming on as
they forced their way into the train.*

Mrs. Wentworth was gently shaking her when she
opened her eyes. "Are you all right, dear?" she asked.

"Yes," said Julie, though she felt empty with fear.
Beyond the window she saw that a lot of time must
have passed. The jungle looked greasy in the late afternoon light.

"You were calling out in your sleep," the Englishman said so quietly that Julie knew he must have
nightmares himself.

She stood up. "I had a dream," she said. "I think I need some air."

She went into the corridor and down the carriage to the little bridge between the cars. Douglas Diamond was there.

"Hello," he said. He seemed more relaxed than before.

Julie leaned against the rail watching the long shining plain of jungle. The air was much cooler than it had been earlier.

"We'll be there soon," Douglas commented. He seemed to have made a decision to be friendly.

"Did you get anything to eat?" she asked him.

He shook his head. "I'm not hungry much." He looked off to where the far hills were tipped with gold as the sun lowered toward the horizon.

Ahead suddenly Julie saw a tunnel approaching. "A tunnel," she said, thinking that they should go inside.

"Yes," Douglas said without looking. "There's one hill before we reach the city."

Julie braced herself for the darkness that was to be upon them in an instant. Without self-consciousness Douglas reached over and put his arm around her, not holding her to him, but making her feel his presence.

The tunnel was much longer than she had expected. The train clacked and clacked over the rails. In the dark, she felt uncomfortably close to the older boy but she didn't want to move. As they approached the other side of the tunnel, there was a wild flapping of wings around the bridge, and Douglas pulled her closer to him.

"A bat," he said to her. His voice, even over the noise in the tunnel, was as unemotional as it had been when they'd met.

Julie clung to him. As the light grew she saw the poor little creature flapping for all it was worth to escape the train. Then they burst out into the light and the bat stayed behind in the tunnel. Douglas let his arm drop.

"They're blind, you see. They can't see the light at the end of the tunnel."

Julie's heart was hammering.

"Look," Douglas said.

Julie saw Kuala Lumpur on the plain below. Down from the hills, the jungle was receding and the town stretched in every direction.

Douglas said nothing, and the fear changed within Julie from one of dreams and darkness to the meeting ahead with her father. She went back inside without thanking Douglas, for his eyes were fixed on the town as though he were trying to memorize its configuration.

The carriage was filled with activity, and by the time Julie had her bags down, they were pulling into the pink stone railroad station.

Douglas appeared in her doorway. "I'll take those," he said. He took the bags and went back into the corridor.

The train had slowed to a stop. With a piercing whistle the carriages jolted and thudded back a few feet in the direction they had come. The passengers began to file out.

Douglas was down first. Julie came at the end. When she stood with Douglas Diamond, most of the passengers had already pushed toward the gates. They were last.

Two men stood waiting for Douglas and Julie—a rather heavy man with intense eyes that Julie could remember from the picture her mother had showed her and another man, just as tall, but much thinner, who stood slightly back and to the rear of the man who was watching Julie.

"My father's come, too," Douglas said to her.

Julie moved forward toward the heavy man. "Daddy!" she called. He didn't move, and she ran forward and threw her arms about him.

"No, Julie," he said quietly, gently pulling her away, "not me."

Startled, Julie looked at him. Now close up staring at his face, she saw that the eyes, though as dark and intense as in the picture, weren't the same at all.

She looked at the thinner man, so thin that he might have not eaten in years and years. His hair, once dark brown, was now the color of salt and pepper.

"Hello, Julie," her father said.

Chapter Six

Julie opened her eyes to the roar of the bombers overhead. Then she saw that she was in her old room at the estate, with the white mosquito net falling like a veil from the coronet of bamboo set in the high ceiling. The world beyond the mosquito net showed her faded images of a tall chest, an armchair, a small night table with her mother's picture a dim ghost, all exactly as it had been when she'd left ten years ago.

The thunderous sound continued even when she was awake. Those weren't bombers coming in off the channel.

The rains had begun.

Julie stirred in the smooth cotton sheets. Her father and the other planters had been waiting for rain.

They had talked of nothing else, it seemed to Julie, since she'd arrived ten days ago.

She wanted to fall back to sleep again, lulled by the old familiar thunder of the monsoon rains. But she heard a faint sound of voices far off in the house and decided she would get up. He had to talk to her soon, really talk to her, and perhaps today with the rains coming down with a vengeance, he would have the time.

She got out of bed, struggling through the mosquito net. The room felt wonderfully cool, almost as cool as England was, after the oppressive heat of the past few days. At times she thought she would literally have to stop breathing: every breath she took seemed to sear the insides of her lungs with fiery hot air.

She put on a light cotton robe that one of the new amahs, hired because Julie was coming to the house, had shyly given her as a gift. The robe, pale green, was emblazoned with a large yellow butterfly that seemed to flap its wings when Julie raised her arms. She loved the robe and lifted her arms to pin her hair behind her head, watching in the long mirror at the farthest end of her room how the butterfly seemed to stir and come to life as though it, too, had just awakened.

The young amah in her white *badju* and black pants was waiting just outside Julie's door. "Missy would like her bath now?"

"No," Julie said, then had to answer much louder over the sound of the rain that had drowned out her voice. "Later."

As she went down the hall toward the living room she wondered how long the young amah had been waiting outside her door. It had taken Julie a while to get used to the old ways, of having people anticipate her wishes and rush to do them before she had even thought of what she wanted. Ten years in wartime England had taught her to cope and to enjoy coping. She couldn't get used to having people wait on her again. It didn't seem fair.

She had never thought about whether it was fair when she'd lived here before. Of course she had been a child then, she thought as she came out of the long hall from the bedroom wing into the wide plain-floored living room with its low rattan furniture.

The living room looked very different now. At first she hadn't been quite sure why. When she did understand, the realization had come as such a shock that she had to sit down in one of the chintz-cushioned armchairs; every detail that her mother had added was gone: the curtains were now plain, the carpet that had once been Oriental, pink and blue, was gone, all the vases that her mother had chosen were gone.

And why not? There had been a war. What had she expected?

The house was like a tomb. Everything was there except the life. Julie pushed that thought away hurriedly. She mustn't think like that. She was home.

Now as she passed across the living room it was as dark as twilight, the rain falling in an unbroken curtain beyond the veranda, the furniture sitting in small ghostly groups. She heard a car engine start and ran the last few feet to the long, deep veranda.

"Daddy!" she called, but the Jeep was maneuvering down the long driveway, around the puddles that were already gathering in the rich, brown mud, and heading toward the distant parts of the estate.

She might have cried except that would have been so...so girlish. She liked being a girl, but she had never, never been *girlish*, which in Julie's mind was defined as being simpering and weepy and generally demanding. She had seen girls like that at school. They had seemed to her like a species from another planet, girls who thought their every wish was some sort of heavenly command to the rest of the world. It had amazed her that they weren't ashamed of themselves.

When the Jeep had disappeared, she went back into the house. Now that she wasn't anticipating talking to her father and her thoughts were more in the present, the rain seemed much louder. She had forgotten how loud the monsoon rains could be. She had thought of them as something like a celebration: everyone, she remembered, wished for the rains to come.

They got short-tempered and snappish with one another because the days before the rains stretched out with unmoving air and terrible temperatures. Then one day the clouds broke overhead and the rains came and everyone went a little dizzy with relief.

She could remember her mother would have an impromptu party when the rains came, calling up all the other planters, those with wives and families and those without, asking them over to the house for a long lunch.

The table had stretched out all down the veranda, with perhaps fifty people counting the children and the bachelors. The rains fell beyond the roof and the lunch got very merry. After lunch Julie's father wound an old hand Victrola and everyone pushed back the furniture and danced in the living room until it was time to go home.

Today the house just seemed suddenly chilly. Julie shivered.

She had come to the kitchen. The cook and his helper looked at her with surprise, and she realized that she had done something she shouldn't: she had walked into their territory, the kitchen, in her robe.

"Could I have my tea now?" she asked.

Confusion reigned as the helper and the cook, both Chinese, for the Chinese worked inside the house and the Malays outside for some reason that Julie didn't understand, ran around the kitchen as though she had accused them of something. The young amah came into the kitchen to see what was wrong, and the cook shouted at her as though it was her fault Julie didn't have her tea.

Julie, on the verge of apologizing, retreated instead to the dim living room. She wasn't welcome in the kitchen, she thought, and she wasn't really welcome out here at all. Her father had practically run away from her this morning, and in the ten days she had been here he hadn't exchanged more than a couple of

hundred words with her. She kept catching him looking at her strangely, almost angrily.

Oh, dear, she thought. I am feeling really sorry for
myself. Get a grip on yourself, girl.

She still was feeling weepy, however, as she went
toward the door to the veranda.

"Hello."

She jumped like a fool, screamed and then stood
feeling absolutely stupid as Douglas Diamond faced
her from the doorway.

"I'm sorry," she gasped finally. She realized now
that she was still in her nightclothes, though she had
thrown the beautiful robe over them. Why, oh, why,
had she decided today to break the routine and come
out into the house in a robe?

"Is your father here?" he asked. Clearly he thought
she was a lunatic.

"No," she said trying not to stammer in her embarrassment. "He went out." Even as she said this,
Julie felt it was a totally inadequate way to describe her
father's leaving in the teeming rain.

Douglas Diamond stepped back away from the
door. He looked taller this morning. His long tropical
shorts and bush shirt were neatly pressed. "I had a
message from my father," he said, looking out into the
rain.

"I could take it," Julie suggested.

Douglas Diamond seemed to consider the idea. He
was very handsome, Julie decided. He looked older
and more serious than sixteen, as though he had
gathered wisdom but it was a burden. His eyes were

shadowed by heavy lashes and there were smudges under his eyes that told of sleepless nights.

He must have dreams, too, Julie thought. Nightmares.

Suddenly she wanted to talk to him. She stepped out into the veranda and said, "I was going to have some tea. Will you stay?"

The rain was her ally. It poured down much louder, lashing the banana fronds of the kitchen garden into shreds. Any answer Douglas might have given was lost in the sound of the rain, and right then the kitchen boy brought out the tea tray.

As Julie gestured to the boy to put it on one of the rattan tables, a part of her mind registered that she was using a gesture exactly like the one her mother had used. She picked up a cup, indicated they needed a second, and the boy left.

Douglas, deciding to stay perhaps because his protests couldn't be heard, drifted to the rail at the edge of the veranda. He sat there looking out at the rain.

When the boy came back, Julie poured tea for them both. She held up the sugar and cream to ask if Douglas wanted either, but he got off the rail and came over to where she was sitting—once again in a position just like her mother's—and reached down to take the sugar bowl. As he did so, his hand brushed over Julie's arm and she had the strangest feeling that no one had ever touched her quite like that, though he had inadvertently just brushed her arm as any stranger might.

She put the creamer down, uncertain whether she wanted him to touch her again even by accident and moved slightly away from him as he put three spoonfuls of sugar into his tea.

As he sat down, the rain—on cue—stopped as though someone had turned off a spigot. Nothing moved, nothing called or cried out. The jungle had been stilled.

"I like it after it rains," Douglas said quietly.

Julie looked at him. She didn't feel it would be right to speak.

"The world seems new," he said, as though to explain his feelings. They became aware of the dripping of the water from the eaves of the house, then other sounds came to them—voices from the kitchen, an impatient chicken squawking in the yard behind the house, distant Malay voices.

"Did you come right back here after..." Julie began, then she blushed because he looked at her as though she had pried. "I'm sorry," she apologized. "I didn't mean to be rude."

His jaw muscles tensed. "No," he said, obviously making an effort to be natural. "That's all right. Yes, we came right back." He looked out at the estate, the rows of even, young rubber trees all fresh as new paint in the aftermath of the rain. "There wasn't anywhere else to go."

"You could have come to England," Julie said. She was thinking, of course, of her own father who hadn't come for her.

"Why?" Douglas Diamond asked, looking at her with his dark, secret eyes.

"It's your home, isn't it?" She leaned forward. "I mean you live out here, but England..." What she wanted to say was what everyone knew. Even if you had been born out here and lived out here, if you were English by birth, then England was your real home.

"I've never been there," he said.

"I know," Julie told him. "I had never been there until..." She stopped, unwilling to bring him pain by bringing up the war.

"It's all right," he said. "You can talk about it. I don't mind."

"Well, I went there when the war came," Julie said, once again feeling like a complete fool. He already knew this. She wished she hadn't invited him to stay for tea. She wished...she wished...she wished she had never come out here, she thought fiercely.

It was the first time she had thought that, though she had been unhappy at the way her father had received her. But now that she had allowed the thought to form, she found she was very angry. "I'm sorry," she said, rising, and once again she could see a distant picture in her mind's eye of her mother doing exactly this.

She felt doubly trapped for a minute, trapped by her journey here and trapped by all these gestures that had come from the past as though a ghost had risen and taken hold of her body.

"I have to bathe and change," she said. But her confusion made her clumsy. As her foot stepped on the pale green robe, she fell forward. The butterfly across her seemed to drop from the air, wings fluttering with panic.

She fell right onto Douglas, spilling his tea all down his shirt and shorts.

"I'm so s-sorry," she stammered as she got to her knees. She felt worse than she could ever remember feeling, awkward, more terrible than at any time except when her mother had died.

Douglas Diamond sprawled beneath her, looking furious. He slid slightly away as though he didn't want to be touched, and Julie started to cry. Not a quiet cry of mortification and embarrassment, but deep, racking sobs.

She felt him move again and she tried to get up, but she was caught with the butterfly in the robe. Then she felt him put his arms around her very gently, almost as though she were a butterfly herself, and lift her up from the floor. She knew he was saying something to her, but her own crying was so loud that she couldn't hear the words. He sat her back on the sofa and perched, lightly for such a large boy, at the edge of the seat, still holding her, though his hands and arms hardly touched her.

The rain started again, very loud. Julie sniffed. She tried to wipe her eyes on the sleeve of the robe, but Douglas picked up a serviette from the tea tray and wiped her eyes as gently as he would a child's.

"Stay here," he mouthed to her over the falling of the rain. He went inside the house.

The rain fell beyond the porch, and Julie sat shivering for a few minutes longer until Douglas came out, followed by the boy from the kitchen. The boy started to clean up the mess Julie had made, while Douglas revealed that he'd found a light blanket. He shook it out like a dark blue cloud and put it around Julie.

They sat across from each other while the rain continued to fall. Douglas stared openly at Julie as though she were some strange rare creature that he had come across in a ride through the jungle, a creature who needed help but might be dangerous. Julie, embarrassed again, was avoiding his glance except for quick, furtive sidelong looks.

Then on one of her quick looks, she saw he was smiling. He really did think she was a child or a fool! She tried to muster some indignation, but she found that she was smiling, too, then giggling, then laughing.

She hadn't laughed in a long, long time. Not like that. Douglas sat looking at her, smiling away, but now with a small frown, too, as though he had been right the first time: she was a little dangerous, and perhaps...

Then the rain stopped again, the way it will do in the tropics as if the heavens themselves know that rainfall there is out of place and must be over and done with as quickly as possible.

To her chagrin, Julie burped.

"Excuse me," she said, flushing again with embarrassment.

"All right," he said, still smiling.

"I don't usually behave like this," Julie said.

He didn't say a word.

"You don't believe me, do you?" she said, feeling some of her indignation come back.

"If you say so, of course I do," he said.

But he didn't. She could tell. "You think I'm a stupid, foolish girl," she said, not as an accusation but as an accepted fact.

He might at least have protested, she thought when he said nothing. The Chinese boy came back with a new cup for him and some cloths to wipe his khaki shorts and shirt. Douglas waved them away. "I'll get much wetter later," he explained. "I'm going out to the river to see if the *kampong* is all right. The rains will start again."

"Why would the *kampong* be in trouble?" Julie asked. She liked the way the word *kampong* came easily to her tongue.

"If the river rises too high it can reach the houses even though they are on stilts," he said. "Then the people sometimes can't get out. They have their livestock in the houses during the rains and sometimes there aren't enough boats. They won't leave, you see, and come inland because it's their home."

There was that word again. *Home.*

He was saying, "They prefer to stay and see if the gods will let them stay in their homes."

Julie had picked up the teapot and was pouring him more tea. "Three sugars?" she asked him.

Now he blushed, just exactly like a naughty boy caught stealing chocolate. "We didn't have sugar in camp," he said.

Julie heaped three spoonfuls into his tea and handed it to him. "We didn't have it in England, either," she said. "Not much, anyway. We had rationing. You got a tiny piece of meat and one egg and a very little sugar, tea and coffee," she said. Then she heard her own words and thought that she sounded as though she were in competition with him. "I'm sorry," she said again. "I don't mean to sound like that. It must have been much worse for you."

He didn't answer her. He looked at the raindrops falling on the blazing spear of the firebushes that rose over the veranda rail. "What was it like—England?" he asked, without looking at her.

"Cold," she said.

His eyes looked at her accusingly. He needed more details.

"It's very different," Julie stammered out, trying to think exactly what England was like. She had lived there for ten years and should have been able to tell him, but somehow she had to get it right for him and she wasn't sure she was qualified to speak for the whole country.

"It's beautiful... and old, but in a nice way... and all the buildings are very solid. Not like this house or the *kampong*. I mean, you have the impression that they've been there forever and some of them *have* been there practically forever, so you feel...very small..." she said. That seemed about right. "I mean everything means something. Everything, roads have had battles, buildings have been lived in by long-dead people..." She stopped. "I'm not very good at this."

"I like to hear you talk about it," he encouraged her. He hadn't touched his tea.

"Well, you feel *small*," Julie repeated, and now she was more sure of what she was saying. "Because so much has already happened everywhere you look. You feel humble," she said.

She was quite pleased with her explanation until he said, "It sounds rather like a prison."

Then she was outraged again for a second or two until she understood that he had spent most of his youth in a prison.

"It's not," she said. "It's very free and very beautiful but in a different way."

"I think I like Malaya better," he decided and raised his cup and drank the tea in one movement as though to close the subject.

The sun came out from behind the thin cloud cover, brilliantly gilding the long sweeps of rubber trees and the jungle that rose to peaks on the far horizon.

On impulse Julie said, "Can I come with you?"

"Where?"

"To the *kampong*. I won't take long to change."

He didn't look pleased. "I'm going to ride."

"I can ride," she reminded him. "I have been riding since I was five."

She could see that he was thinking of an excuse to get rid of her. "All right," he agreed reluctantly.

Julie was on her feet before he could change his mind. She raced through the house and undid her robe as she entered her room. She wished that she had time to bathe and wash her hair. Then she said to her reflection in the mirror, "You are an idiot." Of course it didn't matter to Douglas what she looked like. And when she came back from the ride she would have to bathe, anyway.

"You'll get soaked, in any case," she reminded her image as she quickly pulled on cotton slacks, heavy shoes and a light pink blouse. The crying had made her eyes look large and luminous, not at all a bad effect, she decided.

Chapter Seven

When Julie ran back through the house, she had a strong feeling that Douglas Diamond would have made his escape, leaving her a message for her father. Though not surprised, she felt a sharp pang of disappointment, much sharper than she had expected, when she came out onto the veranda and found it empty. Then she saw Douglas coming round the corner of the house below leading two horses.

The horses in Malaya were smaller than those in England. She had forgotten that. Douglas held the reins of a nice lively chestnut, and Julie swung herself up nimbly just to show him that she could ride well. He got on his own horse, a black mare that backed away a few steps, then impatiently did a little dance as though reflecting her rider's desire to be gone.

They went down the long row of coconut palms toward the direction of the river. Julie could feel her spirits lift as the clouds vanished as though erased from the sky. She knew that the rains could still come back at any moment, but for now the day was bright with sunlight, the sky as blue as porcelain and each leaf and flower sharply defined.

She felt at home. She had felt at home when the plane banked over the island of Singapore and then for a while up here with her father so quiet and changed, she had wished she hadn't come. Now she felt at home again.

"Thank you," she said to Douglas, who was riding with a very good seat, easily moving with the strong haunches of his mount, eyes straight ahead, lost in his own thoughts.

"Thank you for taking me along."

He took a second, but then he smiled, a warm welcoming smile that transformed him into the trouble-free boy he might have been. "You should be able to go anywhere you want," he said. He said it with ease but conviction. "This is your estate."

"I used to think that. When I was a little girl I used to think this was my whole world. I didn't want any other."

He looked around at the trees and the road, at the jungle and the peaks. "You shouldn't want anything else. There isn't anything better," he said. "The difference between people like you and me," he added—Julie felt happy to be included in the comparison—"and other people, people who weren't born here, is that we aren't afraid. There's nothing here to make us afraid.''

''I still am,'' Julie admitted. ''I feel strange, frightened sometimes when I hear sounds I can't identify.''

''It will come back to you,'' he insisted. ''You mustn't be afraid. Not of anything. It doesn't help to be afraid.''

She knew he was talking of far more than the jungle sounds that sometimes came to her across the estate at night: monkeys chattering, the roar of some wild beast, the scream of parrots as they fled for shelter, and worst of all, the terrible mourning silence of the jungle when a kill had been made.

They had come now to the place where the main road out of the estate forked to head toward the river. Birds called to one another from the rubber trees, and the workers, who scored the bark on the trees with their sharp knives, were moving farther down the road.

''Those are old trees,'' Douglas said, as much to himself Julie thought, as to her. ''The newer ones won't give sap for another two years. It takes seven years for a rubber tree to mature, and during the war...''

Julie knew that during the war the estate had been neglected.

''What will you do,'' she asked him, suddenly struck by the thought that Douglas Diamond was almost grown up, ''when you grow up?''

He looked at her with a startled expression, reining in his horse so she backed up a step or two. ''I'll work an estate.''

They rode on a hundred yards, Douglas keeping enough in front of Julie that she couldn't ask any more questions. Finally he began to slow down. He said, when she drew abreast of him, "I want my own estate. My father had one but..." After a second or two he said, looking at Julie with a strange expression, part pain, part trust, "He's not very good as a businessman. He's a fine manager. But he can't run his own business."

"Where will you have your estate?"

"I'm not sure," he answered, relaxing as she didn't pursue his father's past problems as a businessman. "Maybe near here. I like it here."

"It's close to Kuala Lumpur," Julie pointed out, for that's where most of the planters liked to go to relax. There or farther down in Singapore. "Or as close as you can get and have a good estate."

"I don't care about towns," he said angrily. "I like to be alone."

Julie felt as though she had been rebuked. She understood what Douglas was saying. He liked the freedom of the estate. He had lived in the camp close by other people for years and had no freedom. Still she somehow felt that the anger had been directed at her, and she let her own horse drift back as though some type of current was pulling her away from him.

When they came to the fork in the road leading toward the river, he stopped and waited for her. "I'm sorry," he said, shamefaced, holding the reins to his horse lightly over the saddle in one hand.

"That's all right," she told him gently. "I understand why you feel the way you do."

He sighed, looking past her at the distant ridge of hills. "Do you? Sometimes I don't know why I feel the way I do. I feel as though I never want to see anybody ever again."

Julie, without thinking what she was doing, reached out and put her hand over his as he held the reins. He blinked and looked at her with a new expression. She took her hand away.

"In England," she told him, "I used to have to remind myself sometimes that I was one of the lucky people. Others had suffered far worse."

"Yes," he said, but he didn't sound convinced. "We are the lucky ones." He turned his horse down the road toward the river and spurred her first to a canter, then into a gallop that sent mud flying out behind her hooves from the puddles left by the hard, early rain.

Julie followed more slowly. As they drew closer to the river, the rubber trees with their pale trunks thinned and then stopped abruptly. A new vegetation of banana trees, coconut palms and low jungle creepers grew on both sides of the narrow dirt road. Julie saw the thatched roofs of the *kampong* rising above the lowest trees.

They had come to a clearing by the riverbank where a dozen huts sat on tall stilts. Pigs and chickens ran free. Children, many half naked, crouched over their games. Two women tended an open fire. They laughed and talked to Douglas who had dismounted and stood holding his horse by the reins while he conversed in fluent Malay.

The two Malay women clearly knew him and liked him. Though Julie didn't understand the language anymore—she had once had a smattering of both Malay and Chinese—she knew they were joking with Douglas. When she rode into the clearing they looked at her, pointed her out to each other as though she wasn't there, then after another machine-gun chatter of Malay to Douglas, burst into laughter.

Julie blushed. She got off her horse slowly, trying to hold a smile, but the women were shaking their heads, pointing to her again, to Douglas again, and giggling like gossips.

Douglas looked at Julie, made a remark in Malay and the women burst into shrieks of laughter.

Flushing with anger, Julie tied her horse to the nearest tree and walked off toward the river. The children, a dozen or more who had flowed out of the huts, followed her with shy little smiles. "Hello," she said to them.

They put their hands over their mouths, exchanging secret smiles with their eyes. At the river two of the boys took her hand and stood looking at the fishing boats that were pulled up under the arching coconut palms.

Douglas came up behind her. "We weren't laughing at you," he said.

She was still angry. "No?"

"No," he said. "They were saying you were too beautiful for a man like me."

She was struck by the word "man." He was nearly a man. Yet in other ways he was more of a boy than many of the boys she had known in the village back in England where she had spent part of the war. He had had years taken right out of his life.

Letting go of one of the children's hands, she touched her hair. The child took hold of her skirt. She stroked the child's head. "I'm not beautiful," she said. She knew she was pretty, but she didn't think she was beautiful. Her mother had been beautiful.

"I think you're beautiful," Douglas told her.

She couldn't think what to say. She was saved from having to say anything, for one moment she was standing by the riverbank with the dark, muddy river running by, sunlight flecking its brown surface with golden highlights, and the next the rain was pouring down, soaking all of them.

The children ran off shrieking to hide under the huts. Julie felt Douglas grab her hand and pull her to shelter. She ran after him laughing like the children, and they went up the steps to one of the huts. In a second they were within its dark, warm interior. The hut smelled of spices and the rush mats and thatched roof. She could hear the rain pounding on the roof, but within they were alone in a silence that seemed to be a bond between them.

She knew he was going to kiss her, but she had no fear. He moved the few inches forward, still holding her hand, then he put his arms around her very gently, looking into her eyes and she realized that he was nervous, too. Any movement from Julie and he would have dropped her hand and moved away. She was as still as a jungle creature.

Their bodies touched and he leaned down and placed his lips very gently on hers. Julie closed her eyes as happiness broke over her like the pounding monsoon rains over the jungle outside.

Chapter Eight

Did Douglas take you riding?'' her father asked.

The rains had stopped in the late afternoon and she and Douglas had ridden back along the same trails that had led them to the riverbank. The trails had been as deep in water as small streams. On the river the water had risen so high that Douglas had to speak to the head men of the village to point out that the river would soon flow right under the huts of the *kampong*.

"Yes."

"Curious time to go out riding," her father said.

The lights in the house had gone off earlier, and they were eating dinner by hurricane lamps in the long dining room that ran along one side of the house. The lamps, set along the table, gave out a harsh light in two circles but the rest of the room was dim and shadowed.

Julie sat in her mother's chair at one end of the table. She had to look through the bluish white light toward her father, who appeared to her like a stranger in the shadows.

"He was looking for you," Julie said. "He had a message from his father."

"Oh?" her father said, looking at her with a curious birdlike turn of his head. "What was it?"

"He didn't tell me."

Her father held her glance down the table for a long moment. Then he nodded as though at some private thought. "I'll send a boy down to find out later. I expect it had to do with the new trees. This rain will be very good for them."

The rain had stopped some hours ago. Julie and Douglas had ridden back through an estate that glistened with light on raindrops that had gathered in the deep leaves of the banana palms, in pools along the road, on the hibiscus blossoms of the bushes near the house. It would start again later.

At that thought she had to look down at her meal, for she could feel the blush rising in her face. Her throat seemed to constrict as her body remembered the feel of Douglas's hands on her arms and the look in his eyes as he'd leaned down to touch her lips with his.

When she looked up some minutes later, it was to see her father watching her curiously, his knife and fork raised in each hand by his plate as though he had asked her a question while he was eating.

"I asked you where you had gone?" he repeated patiently.

"Oh." She was flustered. "We rode down to the *kampong*. He wanted to see if the huts had been flooded."

The expression on Julie's father's face changed. He almost smiled. "He's a good boy," he said. "He's had a terrible time." That was as close as her father had come in the ten days to talking about the time in the camp. "He'll be a good estate manager one day."

"Is that what he'll do?" Julie asked.

"Yes," her father answered, surprised. "I expect he will. Did he say anything else?"

They were talking like strangers, Julie thought. Polite strangers. She thought of how different her reunion with Spider had been, how emotional. She tried now to remember if her father had been an emotional man. She thought so. She remembered the way he used to take her mother in his arms, the way his eyes used to smile, how lightly he moved on his feet for such a big, strong man. He wasn't strong at all now. Or he didn't look it, anyway. He looked as though he had shrunk in the camp. Yet he had survived three and a half years on rice with hard work, day after day.

And so had Douglas.

"No," she said. There was so much more she wanted to discuss with him. How she wished her Spider were here! Spider would have understood if she had said, "Douglas kissed me." She didn't want to think what her father would say, but she knew enough not to mention it. He might send Douglas away for a while. After all, Douglas's father worked for her own father. Or he might forbid them to meet.

However her father said, "I'm glad you and Douglas are becoming friends."

It was a perfectly normal thing to say, but still she was surprised. She dropped her fork with a clatter on the plate.

Her father seemed not to notice. He said, "He needs to know English children."

Children? She didn't think of herself as a child at all. She felt as though she had passed through some veil of life, like a rainstorm, and stepped out into a new world.

"When he goes home to school, he'll have to learn to get along with children his own age."

"When is he going home to school?"

"You mustn't say anything about this," her father cautioned her. "His father hasn't told him yet. He's going home with you when you go."

Julie felt a great soaring of happiness in her heart, like some wild bird rising out of the darkness of the jungle, breaking into the light and flying free over the unbroken plain. "Oh?"

"Yes," her father said. He hesitated as though he had already said too much. "His father thinks it's best. At any other time... At any other time, he would have been sent home to boarding school years sooner. Of course he'll only be back there a few years now, but it should be enough—" He stopped again, once more uncertain whether to go on.

"Julie," he said, peering at her through the light in the center of the table. "You should be careful with Douglas."

He watched, to see her reaction. "Why?" she asked, and her heart was still and cold.

"He's not . . . He's not like other boys his age. The camp. . ."

"I like him," she said firmly.

Her father sat up straighter, and for a moment she saw him as he used to be—strong, the most decisive man she had ever known. "We all like him," he said. "That's not what I mean."

The outburst just erupted from her without her even knowing what she was going to say. "*All* of us have had terrible experiences," she burst out. "Why can't you see that? I understand what's happened to him, too. You're not the only people who've suffered!"

She jumped up from the table and fled through the house past her startled father and into her bedroom where she flung herself down on her bed.

The servants hadn't yet come in to turn down the covers and lower the mosquito net. She lay there and the tears came in a flood just like the rain. She heard her father come through the house. She knew he was standing right outside her door and she wished him to call to her, but after a while, when her tears had stopped, she heard him go away silently.

She rolled onto her back, looking up into the aureole of the mosquito net. She heard her father's Jeep start up out in the drive and then the sound of it driving away.

She sat up, dried her tears and went out into the empty house. The servants had cleared away the meal. They had gone to their own quarters.

A strange peace came to Julie. She walked out onto the veranda where long moon shadows stretched from the overhanging roof. The half moon threw a pale spectral light over the long, even rows of young rubber trees.

She thought she saw a movement out at the very edge of the grounds around the house, a shadow of a person that was there one moment and gone the next. It might even have been an animal, a tiger, perhaps. They came down from the hills when the rains took a long time to come. They stalked the smaller animals, dogs and cats, a goat or a sheep from the *kampongs* and occasionally a child. They weren't killers by nature. They only killed when they were hungry or old and couldn't find their natural prey.

You couldn't expect people to be what you wanted them to be, Julie thought, peering forward to look into the shifting shadows, any more than you could expect tigers to behave the way you wanted them to behave. The events of their lives, their worlds, made them behave as they did.

Douglas was like a wild creature himself, she thought, and she could feel the touch of his hands, rough from the work around the estate, as they had felt on her arms. Yet they wanted to send him back to England as though he were a normal young boy raised out here! He wasn't like that at all. Too much had happened to him. She called up images of her own school into her mind. To Douglas it would be forbidding and cold. How would he know it was filled with friendly voices and kind teachers?

There was a cry in the jungle and Julie started, facing out into the darkness that fell as a single cloud shadowed the moon. There was a long silence, then the cloud passed and the night was lit by the same half moon again.

She went back inside the house. She knew she wouldn't sleep. Her heart was beating with a regular, excited beat, waiting, waiting... She went through to her own room, undressed and put on her light cotton nightgown. The house servants must have moved like shadows while she was on the veranda, for the bed was turned back and the mosquito net hung in folds.

She climbed into bed, certain she would lie awake tossing for hours, but within minutes she had dropped off to sleep, a sleep stalked by dark eyes that seemed one moment to be the eyes of a tiger lurking in the jungle cover, waiting, waiting...and at other times to be the eyes of Douglas Diamond, watching, watching....

In her dream, she stopped just at the edge of the jungle darkness and called out softly, "Don't be afraid. Don't be afraid."

There was a silence, the silence of the world holding its breath, then a crashing through the underbrush as the creature, whichever it was, tiger or boy, running away, and Julie felt a terrible, terrible sadness that woke her up with her heart hammering in her breast.

Her heart stilled. The hammering was the rain come back. She lay in her warm bed and listened to the thundering above and understood suddenly that she had not dreamed this time of the bombers. She knew with a certainty that her dreams of the bombers were gone. Now she dreamed of tigers in the jungle and awoke to rain on the roof overhead.

She pulled the covers closer and rolled over in her warm bed. Soon she was asleep again.

Chapter Nine

A shaft of sunlight woke Julie. Her eyes opened to find her room filled with the light of morning. She had a terrible feeling that she had overslept, pushed back the covers and slipped under the mosquito net.

Her watch on the night table said it was nine o'clock.

Nine o'clock! She never slept that late.

She felt wonderful, as though she had had her first full sleep in years and years. Taking her time, she ran a bath, dressed and sat before her mirror, brushing her hair. When she came out into the house, she was thinking of Douglas and wondering when he would come to see her.

She saw with a shock that her father was sitting on the veranda drinking tea and looking over some papers about the estate. He looked up at her and said, "Good morning."

"Good morning." She was embarrassed about her outburst. "I'm sorry about last night," she said.

He put his cup down and pushed the papers away from him so they slid onto the floor. "No," he said. "I'm the one who should be sorry."

They were awkward for a second or two until the boy came out of the house. "Missy want more tea?" he asked.

"No, this will be fine," Julie said, touching the side of the teapot. It was lukewarm.

"Bring some more tea, please, Boon," her father said.

"Yes, *tuan.*"

Julie wandered toward the side of the veranda. She knew they were going to have the sort of talk that she had longed for when she'd arrived eleven days ago. Now, somehow, she didn't want to have the talk. Her eyes scanned the edge of the trees where the night before she'd thought she'd seen something move. In the daylight the trees stood like sentinels along the edge of the grass. Were they keeping the jungle creatures away or the people of the estate out of the jungle?

She heard her father sigh and said, "I really am sorry about last night."

He paused. "You look like your mother. You know that, don't you?"

She turned to face her father. "No."

"You do," he said. His eyes moved over her face as though she were a stranger. "You look exactly like her.

I wasn't prepared for that. I expected...something else."

The boy brought the fresh pot of tea, but neither of them made a move to pour it.

Finally Julie said, "Was it very bad in the camp?"

He blinked. Clearly that wasn't what he had expected to hear. "No worse than in other places," he said stiffly.

The anger struck like lightning. "Why won't you tell me anything?" Her voice rose.

He looked away. "Because it wouldn't help." He paused, looked back at her and asked, "What good would it do?"

"It would make me feel closer to you," Julie said. The tears came then and she turned, fighting them off. Voices came to them from the estate and she thought, he's waited here to talk to me, and she felt grateful to him.

She was about to turn and apologize yet again when he began to speak.

"It wasn't so bad at the beginning," he said, speaking in a flat voice as though he were reading a report. "I don't know what I had expected. Fair play, I suppose. At first I was just glad that you and your mother had escaped. I didn't, of course, know where you had gone, or if indeed you had made it out of Singapore. All that...down the peninsula was like another world. The world here was the sight of the army lorries rushing south. I knew we were lost when I saw the army go.

"Still, I thought, we'll put up a last-ditch defense. That was what I had been taught at school. You fought for what you believed in, and somehow it all would come out all right. Now I see that that was balderdash even then. I had read what happened in the First Great War. You won't remember your grandfather. But he fought in it and he told me about the trenches, the mud and the gas and the men dying. Though I knew that it had been a terrible catastrophe I had somehow never taken it in."

He stopped and Julie thought he perhaps wouldn't go on. She kept her face averted from him, hoping that if she didn't look directly at him it might be easier for him.

"I hadn't taken it in," he began, "because I had been so happy. It perhaps doesn't do to be that happy. You have so much to lose. I don't know if you remember how it was when we lived up here before the war."

Julie had to make an effort not to blurt out that she remembered everything, every detail.

"But it was like a small paradise." Another pause. "I loved your mother." Pause. "I didn't know it was possible to love anyone that much. Nothing I've ever read tells you what it is like to really love someone, yet even that isn't the miracle...the miracle is that they love you back. You can't believe it. You think you aren't worthy. You think one day they'll find out what you are really like and then it will be all over.

"But it isn't. Something even more wonderful happens. One day you find out quite differently that they do know you. They know you even better perhaps than you know yourself and they still love you.

"And then something happens right within you. Because you are so loved, you start to want to be worthy of that trust. So you slowly, very slowly, find yourself changing in tiny ways, ways perhaps that no one else would notice except the person who loves you. You start to change not just for their approval but because you want to be worthy of them. Everything else is unimportant but suddenly life seems very easy. You can be fair, unselfish, generous if called upon to be so. All because someone loves you."

He had stopped again, and now Julie risked looking at him. His face looked strained, gray. He was living his experience over again, and Julie who knew about dreams and ghosts said, "Don't, Daddy, please don't."

But he couldn't stop now even if he had wanted to. "The lorries went south with the last of the troops and then the silence came: the men on the estate ran away. You couldn't blame them. It wasn't really their war. Then the planes that had been coming up from Kuala Lumpur stopped coming. The ones from Singapore, of course, had stopped long before. There were precious few of them, anyway, as we know now. Not enough to defend the island. There was this long, long silence and slowly we all gathered here."

He looked around the veranda as though he could still see the planters and their families who had come from all over the neighborhood to wait at the house that had once been the center of their social life.

"We waited and the silence went on and on. That jungle silence, you know," he said, peering at her quickly to make sure she understood. "The land itself seemed to understand what was about to happen, and it seemed, as we waited, as though I had never seen the place before. I couldn't stop walking. I went from room to room. I sat in your room and touched your bed and then I went back to the room where your mother and I had slept and I held to my face her pillow that still had her scent on it.

"Not much time passed. It seemed long, but it was less than a day. The night came on and we tried to make the children comfortable. Douglas was here. I saw then that he was going to be an extraordinary boy. He wasn't afraid. Of course none of us knew then what was ahead."

Once again he stopped. "You can't imagine it. Even if I tell you about it, you won't be able to imagine it."

She could. She thought she could. She saw the way Douglas's eyes looked that night when he'd come up the steps from the beach at Spider's house, the depths of anger in him, the pain, and then she thought of the flash of movement she had seen the night before at the edge of the garden.

"The sun came up across the hills and then the noise came but it wasn't the normal noise of the estate: first the Japanese spotter planes came, and they flew over the house so closely that you could actually see the pilots in their cockpits, then from a long way off you could hear this drone and soon it got louder and the first of the troops came up the driveway.

"They were on bicycles!" he exclaimed, as though the thought still amazed him. "Bicycles! They came down the peninsula on bicycles, and it made this extraordinary humming sound like a horde of locusts descending into the valley.

"When the officers arrived, they came in staff cars, of course."

Julie wasn't sure she wanted to hear any more of this. She had wanted him to take her into his confidence, but now, watching him sitting in the chair with his hands on his knees as though he was being interrogated, she felt guilty and afraid to hear the story of his years as a prisoner.

"Do you want to hear everything?" he asked her as though he had read her mind.

"No," she admitted.

But he wasn't going to let her off that easily. "There was torture," he said.

"I know."

"And hunger. Terrible hunger."

"Yes." She felt she was the one being interrogated now. He had turned the tables on her and she didn't like it.

"First they let us stay up here because they wanted the rubber for the war, but later they took us down to Singapore. They took us in open cattle cars and open lorries. A lot of people died, the women and children particularly. You know what the heat can be like."

"Please stop this," Julie said faintly.

"That was when the most extraordinary people showed their courage," he went on as though he hadn't heard. "People who you had barely noticed at the club or around the village showed true strength and others who you thought would be brave were weak. You learned not to blame them because you knew they couldn't help it. They were the ones who were destroyed twice: the first time by being captured and made prisoners, the second when they had to face the fact that they weren't the people they thought they were.

"Down in Singapore they put us all at first in Changi prison. Then some of us were sent to work on the railroad. Of those who remained, many owe their lives to Douglas Diamond."

"Douglas? He was just a boy!"

"Yes. But at night he would escape under the wires of the camp. You've seen those wires that run along the fields?"

Julie could remember the fields that stretched away from the central prison block as they had looked when she'd driven with Spider to the beach house.

"He was small, you see. And the villagers liked him. So they helped him and they took him fishing with them at night. The Japs didn't interfere with the local fishermen. Douglas brought back food to the camp and many people owe him their lives."

So that was why he returned to the beach below the house where Spider lived! He went back to fish with the villagers who had befriended him.

"I won't tell you what the years were like," her father summed up wearily. "They passed. That is all I can tell you. But through them all each person needed something to live for. Some people lived on hatred and some on their belief in God. I lived because I thought one day I would see you and your mother again.''

And her mother had died while he was in camp.

Julie didn't have to put the thought in words because he looked directly at her as though accusing her.

"It was the final irony, you see. Not like a joke— worse, much worse. I came out. I survived. But your mother had died.''

She might have said many things but chose instead to be silent.

"It wasn't that I didn't love you," he continued when he had his emotions under control. "I do. I did. I always will. But I couldn't face going back to England. I didn't know what to do, so I did what I thought was best for you under the circumstances.''

He stopped for a long time as though following some thought of his own.

"I think that is the lesson we all learned: you can't always control your circumstances, your own life. We used to believe we could, then we found out that everyone is at the mercy of fate. It makes everything look different when you learn that. It makes you feel very vulnerable and . . .''

Julie thought he would say "afraid," because if she couldn't control what was to happen to her, she would have been afraid.

But what he said was, "Eastern."

"Eastern?''

"Yes," he said. "I used to think that England was our home, of course, and everything out here was

foreign, but after I got out of camp I began to understand more about the East. I think perhaps we could
learn something from the East, more than we ever
expected, and that perhaps we do not have all the answers we thought we did."

"So perhaps something good might have come out
of the war?" Julie suggested.

"No!" he said vehemently. "Nothing good can ever
come out of human cruelty. But you can learn from
your mistakes if you are intelligent, which is perhaps
as much as we can all expect in our brief sojourn in
this world."

He wasn't the same man she had known as her father. She wasn't sure what she felt about that. She
knew she admired him. He had the same courage, but
he was changed in some deep, fundamental way. And
she knew, though he loved her and she loved him, they
could never make up the years that they had lost.

She put her head back against the pillar that sup-
ported the roof of the veranda and closed her eyes. In
the darkness behind her eyelids she heard the muted
sounds of the estate: the native voices, the sound of a
dog barking, a horse cantering up the driveway.

She opened her eyes to see Douglas Diamond coming up the long palm-lined drive to the house on his
black mare.

He pulled his horse up short where the driveway
widened into a circle in front of the house. He sat there
staring at her with both his hands resting lightly on the
saddle, as though waiting for her to invite him up to
the house.

Once again the silence drew out, except this time it was with the dark-haired boy and not with her father.

Behind her, her father's chair skidded on the floorboards of the veranda as he stood up.

"Well, then," he said in a voice more like his everyday one than the toneless voice he had used when he'd spoken of his years in camp. "I'll be off. There's a lot to do."

Julie turned. "Daddy..."

He stopped at the top of the steps.

Neither of them knew what the right words should be.

He went down the steps when she didn't speak. He strode off across the lawn, passing by Douglas who sat as still as an equestrian statue of a young general.

When her father had disappeared into the estate, Julie and Douglas sat looking at each other for a few minutes longer, then Douglas very gently spurred his horse forward, ignoring where its hooves dug into the lawn, riding forward step by step until he was just beneath the veranda rail where Julie sat.

"I have something I want to show you," he told her.

Chapter Ten

Julie had never been to this part of the estate. She and Douglas had ridden a long way from the river, moving down a narrow path where the jungle on either side had begun to thin. She saw tiny lady's slipper orchids that grew out of the damp cover of the rock to the left of the trail, long vines that hung like ropes from the tall bare-trunked trees and a second growth of pale greenery under the tallest trees like another entire forest hidden from the distant sky glimpsed high above.

"Where are we going?" she asked.

"Are you afraid?"

Down here under the jungle cover, the day had become twilight. As they moved along Julie could feel the creatures that were hidden all around watching silently as the boy and the girl passed on their horses.

"A little," she admitted.

"You don't have to be," Douglas told her. "You only have to be afraid of places you've never been. I've been here many times." He rode on a few more feet, then he said, "There are tribes living here in the jungle, did you know that?"

"The Sakai," Julie said. She could remember her father talking about them. They withdrew year by year farther into the darkness as civilization advanced.

"Yes," Douglas said, looking high above his head where the tallest trees branched into vibrant growth like umbrellas that shaded everything below.

Douglas spurred his horse. The hooves pounded softly on the dirt path. He disappeared from sight and Julie felt a great fear overwhelm her, but when she pushed her horse to a gallop she found that Douglas had only gone a few yards. He sat tall on his horse in a clearing, looking down the slope of the jungle toward the houses of the estate that appeared as small as dollhouses far below.

"I thought you'd left me," Julie said accusingly.

"No, I would never do that to you." He gestured to the scene below. "We aren't that far away, anyway."

They weren't, yet in the jungle a few yards could be as far away as another country.

"Did you know," Douglas said, "that Sakai live exactly as they did a thousand years ago?"

"I think that's sad," Julie replied.

"Why?"

"Well, civilization has come so far—" she began.

He interrupted her. "I don't think it has," he said firmly. "I think we're just as savage as when we lived in caves."

She thought then of his experience in the camp and what her father had told her earlier. Yes, she thought, he might be right.

"Plane travel," she said, "and telephones, new drugs to make people well."

"It's not enough," he said very surely. "It doesn't count enough for everything we've had to give up." He looked around the small clearing that in itself was unusual, for the jungle usually reclaimed land within a few days, weeks at the most.

"The Sakai come here, don't they?" Julie asked him.

"Does that make you afraid?" He seemed to almost taunt her.

"Yes," she admitted.

"Why? They've never hurt anyone. Never."

"No, but . . . but they're strange."

"Because they want to be left alone to live their own lives?"

He made it sound like an argument. She didn't want to argue with him. She got off her horse, letting it graze freely as she wandered to the edge of the clearing from where she could see all the way to the river.

When he spoke, he was standing right behind her. "I am going to live here forever," he said.

She felt him put his arms around her, and she sighed as though his gesture were the most natural thing in the world.

She laid her head back against his shoulder and felt his lips touch her hair. "I'm glad I came back," she said.

"Do you remember me when we were small?" he asked her.

"A little."

"I remember you," he said.

She turned and he dropped his arms. Up close he seemed to burn with a light of his own. His eyes were as fierce as the sun.

"What do you remember?"

"I remember you had a pink dress with blue and white flowers."

"Yes."

"And I remember you had a bicycle with a bent front wheel. A three-wheeler."

"Yes."

"And I remember that you would eat nothing but fried rice all one spring."

Julie withdrew, standing back. She felt as though she had been spied on. The dress that he remembered had been her favorite as a child, made out of a large piece of material left over from one made for her mother.

"I thought you were perfect," Douglas said, his eyes shining with his own memories.

"I wasn't," Julie said. She wanted to switch the conversation back to something lighter. Without meaning to, she looked quickly back into the valley where the estate looked as placid as a picture. She could see her father's Jeep moving along a back road in the very far distance.

They are all slightly insane, she thought.

She moved away from Douglas. "Why do the Sakai clear this land?" she asked. "Do they have villages?"

"No. They move from place to place. You see they are not like us. They live together with the land. They don't try to capture it."

"Is that what we do?"

"Yes, of course," he replied with certainty. "That's what all those rubber trees down there are: we've captured seeds and planted them in captured land. We-*make* them do exactly what we want, even plants and earth."

Julie sat down near the edge of the clearing. She knew Douglas wouldn't come to her right away, but soon, like a wild creature, he did so. He sat near her, looking at her intensely.

"It's all past. You must know that," she said quietly.

Like a wild thing when someone makes a sudden loud noise, he moved back a few inches.

She reached out to him, touching his knee with her fingertips. "Do you want to talk about it?" she asked.

He didn't say yes and he didn't say no. He just looked right down into the valley.

"If you want to," she said. "I would like to hear about it."

He still didn't speak.

"Were you frightened?" she asked.

"I liked it!" he almost shouted at her. A parrot flew out of the jungle nearby, screaming off across the valley. His voice echoed away and then the silence came.

"I liked it," he said again just as deliberately. His eyes glistened with something very much like tears.

"What did you like about it?"

He licked his lips very quickly, and again she had the impression of something wild, untamed.

"I didn't like it at first," he said. "I was frightened then."

"Everyone was frightened," Julie said. She knew her father must have been frightened, also, though he hadn't said so. Perhaps it was just because they had all been so frightened that they didn't want to talk about it.

"Yes," Douglas agreed, but again she could hear the uncertainty. "Then I got used to it. And then after a while... I liked it."

Julie thought about what her father had told her about Douglas. "I'm not sure that matters," she said tentatively.

He wasn't to be deterred. "When we were free," he said, as though she had accused him of something, "I didn't want to leave the camp."

"It had become your home."

"Yes."

"You knew everything there was to know about it," she continued. "And it was familiar."

"Yes."

She sighed. "I felt like that in England."

"You did?"

She nodded. "Not exactly the way you did, but a little bit. I got used to the night coming and air-raid warnings sounding and all of us going underground to sleep in the tube stations. It was . . . it was like a huge family. At first I couldn't sleep with so many people, and then later, when we moved to the country so I wouldn't be near the bombs, I couldn't sleep because of the silence."

He laughed. "I'm sorry," he said. "I didn't mean to laugh."

Julie smiled. "I'm glad you laughed. You look very. . ."

"Very what?" His long lashes dropped and then lifted again to reveal his eyes filled with mischief.

"You know what you look," she stated, still smiling.

His lips curved very slightly into a smile, but he didn't answer.

"I don't think it matters," Julie said, returning to an earlier conversation, "what people say or think. All I think that matters is what people do."

"And what are you going to do now?" he asked her with the same smile playing over his face.

"I'm going to see if I can make you smile more," she told him. "I like you better when you smile."

He turned away and she couldn't see his expression anymore.

"Shall we get the horses now?" he asked.

They rode home through the shallow light of early twilight. The jungle went a darker green all around, then gray, then black. The afternoon had seemed to pass in one long moment, noon one second, twilight the next.

When they came out of the cover of the jungle, the moon was rising in the east, an orange slice cut neatly in half. Douglas turned his horse toward the house with Julie riding contentedly along beside him. She felt she knew him as she knew no one else. They had talked of so much, sharing the things that they liked. They had asked questions and had been ready to listen to the answers each gave as they had never done with anyone else.

Julie saw her father and Douglas's father sitting on the veranda as they rode up the drive. She knew from the way they stopped talking, watching their children ride toward them through the soft velvet night, that they were wondering where they had been all afternoon.

"I don't think he'll mind," Julie said.

"He doesn't like me to wander off by myself. He's afraid for me."

"You'll have to go off by yourself one day," Julie said.

"Perhaps." He looked around, very tall in the saddle, like a young prince surveying his land.

"When you're at school in England . . ." Julie began without thinking.

He stopped the progress of his horse with a jerk on the reins. "I'm not going to school in England," he said.

Julie remembered that her father had cautioned her not to mention the plans for Douglas. Her eyes, however, betrayed what she knew.

Douglas reined his horse back a step or two. "I'm not going to school in England!" he repeated and his voice had changed. It was hard and angry.

"Maybe..." Julie began searching quickly in her mind for the words to make him understand it might not be so bad.

"I'm not going to school in England!" he shouted at her loud enough to have both her father and his own on their feet up on the veranda.

He turned his horse in one quick movement and galloped it off down the driveway into the black night.

"Douglas!" Julie called after him, but the night had swallowed him, and she knew that, without meaning to, she had betrayed him.

She looked back to the veranda to find her father and Mr. Diamond standing on the steps looking accusingly down at her.

Chapter Eleven

He's gone!"

Julie opened her eyes to a shaft of sunlight that fell through the lattice shutters onto her bed. How late was it? Usually when she awoke the sun was on the other side of the house.

Her father stood beyond the mosquito net. He seemed a shadowy figure, a ghost.

"Douglas is gone," he repeated.

"Gone?"

Inside the net the air was still and hot. She felt choked. She had been dreaming, a slow dream of jungle paths and fleeing figures on horseback. Somehow she thought that she had woken within the dream.

But then her father began to claw at the mosquito net, pulling it away from where it was tucked under her mattress. Fresher air came into the bed and with it her father's arm, which took her by the shoulder and urgently pulled her from beneath the covers.

"Do you know where he is?" he asked.

She shook the last of the sleep from her mind. "No," she said. "He rode off. That's the last I saw of him." Her father looked very worried. "You were there," she reminded him.

She got out of bed and her father turned away as she put on a robe. She tried to gather her thoughts. As she'd said, the last she had seen of Douglas had been the look of shock on his face when she told him that he would be going home to England. Now, belting the silk robe with the butterfly, she recalled as sharply as though it was happening to her again how she had felt a terrible sense of loss, a hatred of herself for betraying him, as she had watched his horse disappear into the falling night.

"Did he go home?"

"What?" Her father looked at the green robe as though he had never seen it before. And then at Julie in much the same way. He started to walk out of her room. "His father's outside. Get dressed and come on out," he ordered her.

She had meant to go out as she was. She understood somehow that she was growing up very fast, yesterday and today. One moment she had been a child allowed to walk anywhere in the house in her night-clothes and now she was expected to dress before she appeared before adults. She sat down on the side of the bed again, listening to her father walk down the hall, then heard his voice as it came to her muffled, talking to Douglas's father.

A few days ago, she had wanted to grow up and be accepted as an adult more than anything in the world, except a gesture of love from her father. Now she wished she could turn time back.

Slowly she unbelted the green robe and let it drop to the floor with a fluttering of the butterfly's wings. She dressed quickly in a cotton dress, washed her face and went out through the house to the veranda.

Douglas's father was sitting there looking drained of all emotion. "He's gone!" he said accusingly to Julie in almost exactly the same tone her father had used.

She was irritated, angry that they would blame her for this. "You should have told him about England," she said reproachfully.

Douglas's father and her own exchanged a look that said as eloquently as though they had spoken aloud, She's a fool.

"You don't understand, Julie," her father said quietly.

"No?" she demanded angrily. She could see the houseboy coming through the house carrying a tea tray for her. At the raised voice, he hesitated and stood stock-still in the shadowed living room waiting for the owners to stop arguing.

"What don't I understand? That you were all prisoners? That you all had a terrible time?" She sounded as though she were laughing at them and modified her voice. She gestured to the houseboy to come on out of the house and turned away and tried to collect herself.

When she heard the boy going away, she turned back to her father and Mr. Diamond and said, "You treat the rest of us as though we were on a holiday! You treat us like lepers because we weren't in prison camp with you. We had lives, too!" she almost shouted, then in a lower tone she added, "We lived every day, too..."

Her father and Mr. Diamond were exchanging that look again. Sighing, she said, "Did he leave a note?"

Mr. Diamond shook his head. "That wouldn't be his way. Since the camp... where did you go yesterday?" he asked her.

"Riding."

"We know that, Julie," her father told her. "Where, exactly?"

"Is his horse missing?" She didn't want to tell them about the clearing above the estate. She had betrayed Douglas once. She knew they would be looking for him.

"No," his father admitted.

"Then he can't be very far away," she said.

There was an uncomfortable moment, then her father said, "Julie's right, Lou. He can't be very far away. He knows his way all around the estate and the surrounding area. He'll come back in his own time."

"He'll stay away until it's too late to go back to England," his father predicted.

"There are other planes," Julie's father remonstrated. "He doesn't have to go with Julie."

Lou Diamond sighed. "No," he said. "But I thought..." He looked at Julie. "I want him to be happy. Understand that. The camp is over. He has to learn about real life. He can't run away from it forever."

She crossed to where Douglas's father sat looking large and defeated and said touching his strong forearm, "He'll come back when he's ready. He's not ready yet."

Lou Diamond stood up. "The world doesn't wait for us, Julie," he said. "We would like it to, but it doesn't."

He nodded to Julie's father and left. Julie saw the dark, wet sweat stain down the back of his shirt as he went down the steps. The air was still and hot again, waiting for the skies to break with another rain.

Her father said, "You know where he is, don't you?"

"No," she said.

"If you do, you're not helping him any by hiding him." He waited to see if his words would have any effect and when they didn't, he said, "I think you had better go back to Spider."

Chapter Twelve

Julie's father stood at the station, small and straight, the marks of the camp on him in his drawn features, his prematurely gray hair. How different he looks, she thought, from the picture that her mother had kept by her bed all those years.

The train began to move, and Julie wanted to jump up and run down the length of the carriage, throw open the door and call, "Don't send me away!"

The clacking on the rails grew more insistent. Her father watched the train pulling away from the platform. Behind him the station began to fill the window: the pink walls, the arched doors, the domes and minarets. He had become a tiny figure, the station a stage set, as the train gathered its full speed heading south along the peninsula toward Singapore.

Julie wished she hadn't come to Malaya. She had looked forward so much to returning to the estate, to seeing her father. Now, as she pressed her face against the glass, watching the last of the buildings on the outskirts of the town pass the window, she understood that her dreams of what it would be like when they met again after ten years had been unrealistic...childish.

She wasn't a child anymore, she thought sadly. Yet another feeling rose in her at the same time, a feeling that made her reach up and brush the tips of her fingers across her lips.

Douglas would be up in the clearing, she thought. They wouldn't find him. The only people who would find him would be the Sakai and they wouldn't hurt him. They lived peacefully in the jungle among themselves, receding year by year deeper into shadow and darkness as civilization approached.

The town dropped behind the train. Julie felt numb. She closed her eyes and tried to sleep.

The lights of the coastline twinkled in the night as the train slowed to cross the causeway. Julie gathered her belongings. She had slept for a few hours and felt refreshed.

On the other side—on the island of Singapore—the train gathered speed, and soon they were drawing into the station.

Spider was on the platform. She moved down the length of the train while it slowed, searching for Julie.

"Aunt Spider!" Julie called. "Here!"

"What happened?" Spider asked, rushing up to Julie and grasping her by both shoulders. "Are you all right?"

"I'm fine, Aunt Spider," Julie said, kissing her. She tried to move them both toward the gate.

Spider clung on to her arm as the crowd flowed around them. "I knew I should have gone up there with you. I knew I should. But I thought after all this time..."

They were off the platform and in the main part of the station. Julie looked around with relief. "Is the car outside?" she asked.

"Yes, yes," Spider said.

They hurried through the station and into the warm night outside. The long black car with its tall, square corners sat at the curb. The *sais* held the door open for them and soon they were gliding away from the station.

"*Something* happened," Spider said.

"Yes," Julie admitted.

"What? Did you talk to your father?"

"No, not exactly," Julie said. She was watching a tri-shaw—a three-wheeled bicycle pulling a rick-shaw—carrying a large Chinese woman and two children. The tri-shaw driver was as thin as a stick. The woman shouted at the driver, who stood on his pedals pushing down as hard as he could.

"He told me about the camp," Julie said, without looking at her aunt.

"Everything?"

Julie looked at her. "I don't know."

Now her aunt looked away. "They tortured him. Did he tell you all about that?"

"Not really." Julie felt terrible. She had judged and abandoned her father without ever fully knowing what had happened to him.

"They thought he had some information about the rubber. They believed that there were vast supplies hidden somewhere. There weren't, of course," Spider said as they passed the darkened building of the courthouse with its impassive, uncaring facade. "But people who are engaged in subversive things often believe others are doing the same." She looked directly at Julie in the dark interior of the car. "That's why people are so cruel. It's like an accusation to see someone who is good if you're not good yourself. And your father is a good man."

Julie was miserable.

Spider took her hand. "He won't blame you, whatever happened up there. But I've noticed that when people accuse others, it's often because they themselves are guilty of something. I dismiss almost everything that I'm told now that I'm getting older, and it's only the silences that make me wonder."

"What did they do to him?" Julie asked.

Spider sighed. "If I tell you," she said, "you perhaps won't believe me. I think that perhaps that's the worst thing about the war. I think that may be why so many of the people who survived the camps don't want to talk about them: it's incomprehensible sitting in this very comfortable car, riding home to dinner to

1. How do you rate: _____
   (Please print book TITLE)

   1.6 ☐ excellent   .4 ☐ good   .2 ☐ not so good
   .5 ☐ very good   .3 ☐ fair   .1 ☐ poor

2. How likely are you to purchase another book:
   in this *series*?   by this *author*?
   2.1 ☐ definitely would purchase   3.1 ☐ definitely would purchase
   .2 ☐ probably would purchase   .2 ☐ probably would purchase
   .3 ☐ probably would not purchase   .3 ☐ probably would not purchase
   .4 ☐ definitely would not purchase   .4 ☐ definitely would not purchase

3. How does this book compare with romance books you usually read?
   4.1 ☐ far better than others   .4 ☐ not as good
   .2 ☐ better than others   .5 ☐ definitely not as good
   .3 ☐ about the same

4. Please check the statements you feel best describe this book.

   5 ☐ Realistic conflict   18 ☐ Too many foreign/unfamiliar words
   6 ☐ Too much violence/anger   19 ☐ Couldn't put the book down
   7 ☐ Not enough drama   20 ☐ Liked the setting
   8 ☐ Especially romantic   21 ☐ Made me feel good
   9 ☐ Original plot   22 ☐ Heroine too independent
   10 ☐ Good humor in story   23 ☐ Hero too dominating
   11 ☐ Not enough humor   24 ☐ Unrealistic conflict
   12 ☐ Not enough description of setting   25 ☐ Not enough romance
   13 ☐ Didn't like the subject   26 ☐ Too much description of setting
   14 ☐ Fast paced   27 ☐ Ideal hero
   15 ☐ Too predictable   28 ☐ Slow moving
   16 ☐ Heroine too juvenile/weak/silly   29 ☐ Not enough suspense
   17 ☐ Believable characters   30 ☐ Liked the subject

5. What aspect of the story outline on the back of the cover appealed to you most?
   31 ☐ location   32 ☐ subject
   33 ☐ characters   34 ☐ element of suspense in plot
   35 ☐ description of conflict

6. Did you feel this story was:
   36.1 ☐ too sexy
   .2 ☐ just sexy enough
   .3 ☐ not too sexy

7. Please indicate how many romance paperbacks you read in a month.
   37.1 ☐ 1 to 4   .2 ☐ 5 to 10   .3 ☐ 11 to 15   .4 ☐ more than 15

8. Please indicate your sex and age group.
   38.1 ☐ Male   39.1 ☐ under 18   .3 ☐ 25-34   .5 ☐ 50-64
   .2 ☐ Female   .2 ☐ 18-24   .4 ☐ 35-49   .6 ☐ 65 or older

9. Have you any additional comments about this book?
   (40)_____
   (41)_____
   (42)_____
   (43)_____
   _____
   _____

Thank you for completing and returning this questionnaire.

NAME _____
　　　　　　(Please Print)

ADDRESS _____

CITY _____

ZIP CODE _____

remember and actually *believe* what was done—what one human being could do to another, one nation to another.

"And that's not the worst of it. You think during the war that it's just one group. You hate them and you believe that they are evil, but later...." She stopped, lost in her own thoughts while they passed the airport and headed down the darkened road to the sea. "Later you think that perhaps everyone, all human beings including oneself, are capable of such evil and that's worse...much worse." Her voice faltered.

"Don't tell me if it makes you too sad," Julie said. She put her arm about her aunt and laid her head on her shoulder.

"They stopped finally," Spider said. "They just lost interest. You have the most terrible feeling of vulnerability when you are at the mercy of people who can kill you or spare you simply because they are bored, or it's time for lunch. Life has no meaning, it would seem, none. You are worthless."

"He didn't tell me," Julie said.

"No, of course he wouldn't," Spider said. She turned with an anger that shocked Julie. "You all want to *know*. You want us to tell you things. You want to know what happened. It's like being in the camp again, watching him being tortured. You have no *right* to know!"

Julie moved away, shocked by the sudden explosion of anger.

Spider composed herself. "Forgive me," she said, in a small voice. Julie saw the *sais* watching her aunt in the rearview mirror with kind, concerned eyes. "I didn't mean that."

Julie felt drained, exhausted. She wanted to go...where? She had thought this was where she wanted to be. She had lived for the time she would come back here. Now she thought of what it would be like when she went back to England. She didn't belong there, either. Would she be like this her whole life, going from place to place, from one group of people to whom she was somehow connected, to another and never belonging—properly belonging—to any of them?

"It's all right," she said dully.

"Of course it isn't," Spider said, wiping her nose with a tiny square of handkerchief she had taken from her bag.

They were passing the wire fences of the prison now. She didn't look at the dark fortress brooding across the empty moonlit fields.

"Do you think it will ever be over?" Julie asked her as the car turned down the road to the beach house.

"No," Spider cried. "It mustn't be over! You want to forget it. We understand that. You want to pick up life as it was but we can't..."

"And so *we* can't," Julie said.

"Do you want to?" Spider asked.

"I want to go on," Julie said. "I want to live my life. I can't change the past. None of us can."

"If we forget, then all the ones who didn't come back will count for nothing," Spider said stubbornly.

The car passed through the gates to the house. The avenue of frangipani trees glowed with a milky light fallen from the almost full moon onto the flesh-white blossoms. Their perfume filled the car.

"We are our memories," Spider murmured.

Julie felt dizzy from the sweet scent of the avenue of flowering trees and from the long journey in the heat of the night. Her aunt's words seemed to ricochet through her skull.

"Memories don't have to control us," she said. "We can be more than just what we remember."

"Why should we be?" her aunt demanded. "Youth...you have rules for all of us, but you haven't lived at all...."

"We have lived through the same years you have!" Julie said angrily. She was tired of adults, tired of the past, tired of Singapore, Malaya...all of it. "The years I have been alive are the same years you've lived for the past fifteen years. You want me to believe that I don't have a right to my own beliefs because you're older, but I have memories, too—memories that are as strong as yours. I think you're all selfish."

"Selfish!" Her aunt was shocked.

The car had stopped at the steps up to the terrace in front of the house.

Ah Foon was coming out of the wide front door. The *sais* sat still, unspeaking, unmoving, in the front seat.

"Selfish," Julie reiterated emotionlessly. "You want to believe your war was worse than everyone else's.

You want to be quiet and noble and suffer publicly forever like some stage characters.''

"Be quiet, Julie! You don't know what you're saying!"

"Well, I think you were lucky," Julie said. In her heart she was as shocked as Spider, recoiling into her corner of the car, at her words.

"Lucky!" Spider gasped.

"Yes," Julie whispered. "You had one another. I had Mother. Then I had no one."

Ah Foon had come to stand at the top of the steps. She seemed to understand that this was not a time to run, smiling, to the car. She waited in the moonlight. The *sais* seemed to have stopped breathing.

"What is it you want?" Spider asked.

"I want you to believe that my life is important, too," Julie told her. She was going to cry herself now, but she was determined not to, not just now. "I want you to respect my life, too. This is the only life I have. I didn't make the war, and now that it's over, all any of you want to think about is the past and the war. I feel . . . I feel forgotten, as though my life is unimportant, as though I came along too late to matter to anyone. . . ."

Ah Foon had begun to move down the steps. The *sais* moved his head, shaking it silently at Ah Foon. Then he got out without a word. Aunt and niece sat in silence in the car. The *sais* stood by the darkened headlights looking at Ah Foon on the steps, who stopped and waited.

"You are right, of course," Spider said finally. "We're all locked in another prison now just as much as we were in the camp. Our memories have imprisoned us."

"I love you, Spider," Julie said. "I love my father. But I don't seem to be important to you because I wasn't there. You shut me out." She was still near tears. It was hard to speak the words.

"We do love you, Julie. It's just . . ."

"Don't say whatever you're going to say," Julie said. "I don't want to be someone you love despite everything that's happened to you. . . . I want to be . . . Julie."

Her aunt turned to look at her as though for the first time in her life. "Can you forgive us?" she asked.

"I don't want to forgive you," Julie answered. "I don't want you to have to understand me. I don't want any of that. I just want . . . you. Both of you. That's what I want." Then because it seemed so clear suddenly, she added, "I don't want any more words."

She thought of Douglas. He didn't have many words, but she felt much closer to him than she did to anyone else. Her mind seemed to float free of her body. She seemed to be above the tiny, enclosed scene in the car. For the first time someone other than her own family seemed more important to her than anyone else in the world.

She imagined that Douglas was nearby. She almost could feel the way his arms had felt when they were around her, the way his lips had felt when he had kissed her. She remembered his expression of concern when he'd looked at her.

She shivered violently.

"You're tired," Spider said.

They got out of the car and walked past the *sais* who looked at each of them with worry in his eyes. "It's all right," Spider told him. "You can put the car away now."

Ah Foon began to chatter, her gold teeth gleaming in the moonlight, as they came up the steps. "Dinner ready, mem."

"Would you like to wash up first, Julie?" Spider asked her in a normal voice, quite as though the long, heated talk in the car had happened days, even weeks, ago.

"Yes," Julie replied, surprised to find that she could summon up a voice just like her aunt's. She was passing into the adult world, she knew, learning all the mannerisms, all the little deceptions that make real life bearable.

She didn't know if she wanted to learn all this. Douglas, with his stubborn refusal to be what everyone wanted him to be, would have understood, she thought. She wished he were here so she could talk to him, and again she had the strangest feeling of his presence nearby.

She went into the house and up the outside staircase to the room that had been given her on the second floor. Up here she had a large bedroom and a wide terrace that took in all the roof above the living room below. She could see the beach and the oil-black water streaked with silver lines etched by moonlight, and over in the distance the pinprick lights of Jahor.

She washed her face, then on impulse took a bath. She knew they would be waiting for her below, but she needed some time to herself.

When she came out of the bathroom, her suitcase was already unpacked. She changed into a clean white dress, noticing in the mirror that she had changed in just twelve days: she looked older, more poised. She almost looked beautiful, she thought with more curiosity than vanity.

Out on the terrace beyond her room, she took another moment to compose herself before she went downstairs. The moon was almost full and very high in the sky tonight, making the world like the inside of a black pearl. She saw that the fishing fleet had left the shore while she was bathing and now was clustered like a group of tiny gems set in the blackness of the sea.

She watched the boats, each with its lamp stuck out behind it on a pole. The figures from this distance were shadows moving on the little boats. She leaned on the terrace wall and looked into the darkness but she could not make him out.

He was out there. In her heart she knew it. If he wasn't yet, then he was on his way. The lights on the boats moved on the tide, swirling in a tiny dance beneath the light of the moon.

Somewhere in the night Douglas was waiting and watching, as she was waiting and watching. If he didn't come tonight, he would come another night. Soon. All she had to do was let him know she was here and then wait for him.

Chapter Thirteen

He didn't come on the first night, nor the second, but on the third she saw a light detach itself from the cluster around the fishermen's nets and head slowly for the shore.

She had been standing at the end of the living room watching for him. In the three days Spider and she had drifted apart as the light was now drifting away from the fishermen. They had become like strangers, polite and distant.

"I think I'll go to bed now," Julie said, turning from the sight of the solitary light trailing its wake of phosphorescence toward the beach.

"Now?" Spider asked. She had been pretending to read a book, but Julie had watched while she read the same page several times.

"I'm very tired," Julie said.

Her aunt allowed her glasses to slide down her nose. "Your father will be calling soon," she said, worry on her face.

"Yes, I know." Julie had to make a decision. Her father had called the first night she had arrived. The conversation had been stiff. He wanted her to take a few days with Spider and then return to the estate.

"I'll think about it," Julie had told him, still vibrating with the emotion from her long, emotional talk with Spider in the car.

"The rains will stop soon," he had said, his voice thin on the long-distance line from the estate.

They wouldn't. They would go on for weeks yet. But she knew he was trying to find a reason for her to come back.

"Why don't you just have a few days on the beach," he'd suggested, trying to get into his voice all the false good humor that many people thought went with being a father. "Then come back and we'll put you to work on the estate."

"Is there any sign of Douglas?" she had asked.

"No. But perhaps he will turn up. In the meantime, will you think about coming back? I don't feel we had a proper talk...."

After her conversation with Spider, Julie wasn't sure at all that she wanted to talk with any of her family anymore. She wasn't at all sure she wanted to go back to the estate. The thought frightened her. If she didn't belong with her father, or with Spider, where did she belong?

"I'll think about it," she'd promised him. But she had seen the light on the water and it haunted her.

"He'll want to know if you're going back," Spider had told her.

Julie wanted to say "Spider, he's coming for me." She wanted someone to talk to, a friend, but she knew that there wasn't time. If she turned right now she would find the light had disappeared beneath the night shadow of the cliff.

"I think I might go home to England," Julie said.

Spider's hands dropped from where they held her glasses on the cord about her neck into her lap. They turned each other over and over like tiny creatures wrestling. "Oh, my dear," she said. "Your father will be so disappointed."

Julie wished Spider would leave her alone. Julie knew that the boat would be almost to the shallows and once there, Douglas would come ashore, come up the steps to the garden and through the garden on his way to the same paths he had followed as a prisoner escaping for one night of freedom.

"I don't think I belong here," Julie said. She didn't want to hurt her aunt. She didn't want to hurt anyone. But she saw how Spider's face twisted with pain as she looked at her hands.

"Life used to seem so simple" was all she said.

The sense that she had to rush from this room, the house, to meet Douglas was overpowering Julie. She could feel his presence as though he were calling to her, as though he were standing right outside the window.

She dropped quickly to her knees. She put her hands on Spider's to still their restless turning.

"Spider," she said, looking up into the small, lined face now contorted with pain. "Sometimes there's nothing people can do."

Spider shook her head just like a child denying what it doesn't want to hear. "You don't understand...."

He would be touching the sand with the bottom of the sampan now.

"I do, Spider," Julie said gently. "I do understand now and perhaps I was wrong in the car."

Spider's eyes widened. "No," she said. "You weren't wrong." She sighed. "It's so hard. I thought when the war was over, it wouldn't be so hard." Her eyes looked beyond Julie to night sky spangled with stars. "It must count for something! Do you see that? It must all count for something. Otherwise..."

Otherwise all life had no meaning, everything was just a child's game, win or lose.

"It does, Spider," Julie told her holding the small hands tight. She didn't know where the words came from, but they came with conviction from deep within her.

"But not everything has to count exactly. It counts, for us, for... for the Japanese..." Spider reacted, trying to pull away... "We're all tied in this together somehow, and it counts but we can't hold on to every loss, to our own losses above everyone else's or... or life would stop."

Julie let go of the hands and they were finally still. "You're wise," Spider said, looking at her niece.

"No," Julie said. "I think people get pushed on stage. That's what I think. I think all of us…everyone involved in the war and afterward…have been pushed onto a huge stage whether we want to be there or not. That's why it sometimes seems so much like a dream. We didn't choose to be here but now we are, we have to speak our lines or everything will stop, and that would be worse."

She got up. The sense of Douglas's presence was fading. She should have run from this room minutes ago. She had been faced with another choice…so many choices…and she had chosen to stay and comfort Spider.

"I'll go now," she told Spider.

Spider let her get to the door. "Julie…"

Julie turned.

"You are magnificent." Her aunt told her. "Just like your mother."

When she was out of the room, Julie ran. Her heart told her that he had come, found that she wasn't there waiting for him, and disappeared into the night and whatever other life awaited him.

But she ran, anyway, out of the house and across the terrace, into the garden where the gardenia blossoms filled the night with their seductive scent and then to the top of the steps. She peered over, looking for the boat, but the beach was a pale yellow crescent in the moonlight, empty, with the water lapping gently on the sand.

A shudder went through her whole body. Loss rose like a tide to take her, and she felt the tears come to her eyes. She had stayed. He had come. Now he was gone.

She took a step down to the beach, then another. She knew she would feel the loss forever. She would make the "right" choices, do the "right" things, she would be thought of as "magnificent," but the rest of her life she would walk with the sense that a ghost walked beside her.

At the beach she looked out at the small group of lights reflected on the water. She could walk right into the dark water, walk out there, until the water rose to cover her.

She shook away that thought...if her mother, whom she had loved so much, had endured, then she could. Whatever life had ahead for her, she could meet it. Spider had said there had to be a reason, searching for each reason for each loss; but Julie knew that the reason might simply be that God expected everyone to go on. Life wasn't a single moment, a week, a month or even a year, years... It was much much more important than that and perhaps no one could ever know why things happened, to yourself or to anyone. You had to trust and go on.

And then the skin along the back of her neck seemed to shrink and she stood rigid, looking out at the water, knowing with certainty that she wasn't alone on the beach.

When his hands touched her shoulders she just stood there, watching how the moonlight traced a crayon path from the far shore to right where her foot was pressed in the sand and the smallest waves lapped at her feet.

"I couldn't go without seeing you," he whispered.

Chapter Fourteen

Douglas stood in the prow of the boat pulling them from the shallows. The sampan had been pulled up in the lee of the cliff hidden by the overhanging vines. Julie watched the fronds of the coconut palms become smaller against the night sky as the shore receded.

When they were in deeper water, he drew the pole in and put it in the bottom of the boat. The fishermen's lights had drifted on the tide, dragging their nets like a train, trawling for their catch.

Douglas sat in front of Julie, his chest bare, his waist wrapped in a long sarong like one of the natives. Around his head he had a piece of batik cloth wrapped to make a turban. He looked like a stranger, yet at the same time he looked more perfectly himself than he had on the estate, dressed like other boys from his station in life.

"Come with me," he had said on the beach as he released her.

She had followed him down the beach to the sampan and when he pushed it out into shallow water, she waded up to her knees in the warm water, climbing in without a word.

Now they floated on the tide, Julie at the stern of the small boat, Douglas in the bow. He took out the oars and put them in their locks, leaning forward to draw strength, then pulling back, the muscles in his chest taut as he pulled stroke by stroke farther from the shore.

Soon they were down the length of the island, drifting completely away from where Spider's house was, from the other shore across the strait. The wind freshened as they came to more open sea. In the very far distance Julie saw the red and green running lights of a freighter making for the ocean. The fishermen's lights looked like fallen stars tossing on the waves they had left behind.

"I used to come here when I was in camp," Douglas said, his voice surprisingly loud and intimate in the emptiness of the sea.

"I know. My father told me."

"The fishermen like to stay in the strait," he continued, as though he hadn't heard her. "The fish come down the length of the island and they don't have to go far out to sea to catch them. They can just wait there with their lights. But I like it out here. It's free."

The emptiness stretched on every side and then suddenly, out of the darkness, a form loomed right out of the sea and Julie screamed, a tight scream from low in her throat, thinking that they had come upon a ship running without lights in the night.

Douglas kept drawing on his oars. Then she saw the large, dark silhouette rising, rising. It seemed to be a kind of island—no, not exactly an island but more of a rip in the fabric of the sea. There was a line of sand, quite narrow, and no trees, just the sand, then on the other side another row of white-capped breakers.

"It's a reef," he told her as he drew the oars in and let the boat be taken by the tide. "It must have risen right out of the seabed at one time." Douglas jumped overboard, up to his waist in the water, and began to haul the boat ashore as the current took them abreast of the small reef that was no longer than fifty feet and no wider than ten.

Julie stood up to crawl forward, then she, too, was over the side, dropping into water that was deeper than she had expected. She helped him pull the boat onto the safety of the sand.

Douglas brought the sampan to the middle of the sandbar. "The water covers everything at high tide," he said.

Out here, facing away from the island, they might have been standing on the water itself. The air was warm and a mixture of spices and the perfume of flowers came to them on the breeze.

"Thank you for coming back for me," she said.

"I thought you had run away from me."

"*Everyone* thought *you* had run away," she said.

"I did."

She waited a moment more, uncertain whether to bring up what had happened. She wanted to be rid of the past. She wanted to walk on into the future, as free as the breeze that came from shore. "I wasn't hiding anything from you," she said. She wanted him to understand she hadn't been in collusion with the adults.

"I know," he said. "It wouldn't matter, anyway." He turned away to look out to sea where the freighter was lost in the night. "I know you can't run away. In my heart I know it." He looked at her quickly. "Do you sometimes lie to yourself?"

"No," she said. "What do you mean?"

"I dream," he told her urgently, taking half a step forward. It was important to him that she understand. "I pretend."

"Oh, I dream a lot, too," she said. "I used to dream about the past all the time."

"No," he said, "I don't mean that. I pretend all the time. I started to do it in camp. I would escape at night and come out onto the sea and I would pretend that none of it, the war, the camp, none of it had happened and I was all alone in the world and there wasn't anybody else. Nobody."

"There will always be people," she told him, allowing some of her sadness to show in her voice.

"I wish there weren't," he said fiercely. "I wish there was just you and me."

She reached up and touched his chest very softly. "There can be," she told him quietly. "That's what love means. Two people make their own world together." She looked at the sandbar beneath their feet where the tide was coming in.

The tide had risen with the dawn when Douglas and Julie headed for shore.

Julie lay back in the boat, watching how the sky paled to purple, then gray, flushed to rose and pink as though embarrassed by the sturdy light of the sun after the gentle light of the moon, then became as white as the interior of a large pearl.

Douglas rowed strongly and steadily. The rows of trees, very small at first, took on silhouette and definition, becoming coconut palms along the shore, bananas inland. The houses took shape out of the greenery.

As they came under the cliff face of Spider's house, Julie saw her aunt standing on the high terrace outside the room that she had given to her niece, watching them.

Douglas rowed them around the headland and then there was the beach, bright yellow in the morning light.

By the time they reached it, Spider had come down from the house. She waited where the coconut palms arched over the sand, throwing faint shadows in the cool morning sun.

When Julie got out of the boat, Spider came into the light.

"Douglas came back," Julie said, as though that explained everything.

"Hello, Douglas," said Spider.

"Hello, Spider."

"Breakfast will be ready," Spider said, as though she came down to the beach every morning to find her niece rowed ashore by a half-naked boy.

Douglas pulled the boat to safety, then Spider put an arm around Julie and Douglas and they moved toward the steps.

For a few moments they all walked in a silence broken only by the lapping of the incoming tide.

Then Spider dropped her arms and turned to look at the beach, the bay and the sun that blazed like a ruby above them. "When I first came here as a young girl," she said wonderingly, "I thought this was the most beautiful spot in the world."

She turned back to Julie and Douglas and linked arms with them again. "You have given me back my eyes," she said. "I shall always be grateful for that."

Chapter Fifteen

The plane sat in the hot sun with its doors open, waiting.

Douglas turned to look at his father with a look of panic. "Papa..." he said.

"Go, Douglas," his father said gently.

Spider, waiting with Julie's father in the shade where the airport building had a small overhang, turned to Julie and said, "You'll look after him, won't you?"

Julie felt a great sense of pride that Douglas, so handsome and in his own way, strong, was being entrusted to her care. She felt a part of Singapore and Malaya, the estates—and in a way the future, too—that she hadn't felt before. "Yes," however, was all she said.

Douglas looked at Julie. She leaned quickly to kiss her own father. He held her to him a few more seconds than she had expected, then, still with his hands on her shoulders said, "I'll be in England for Christmas."

"I'm glad," she smiled. "I'll look after you, too."

"I'll need it." They knew each other much better now. Another month had passed since he'd come down from the estate to talk to Julie after Spider called. They didn't know each other, either of them, in the way they had expected. Somehow she wasn't a daughter—not the way most people were—and he wasn't a father in the normal way, either. They were more like friends, companions, people with memories that bound them together. But they liked each other, too, and that was almost more than she had hoped for.

Sometimes, Julie thought, you had to give up one dream to find another.

"And you and Douglas will both be back next summer for the long holiday," Spider chimed in.

Julie didn't know what she could say to Spider to tell her how much she loved her. It had been Spider finally who had drawn all of them together: Julie and her father, Douglas and Douglas's stubborn father.

So Julie just hugged her aunt and whispered, "Thank you."

Spider, looking into Julie's eyes said, "Keep him safe."

The loudspeaker was calling the departure of the plane. All the passengers were on board. Julie looked at Douglas and, though she thought she might embarrass him, took his hand. They started off across the sun-seared tarmac toward the ramp leading into the British Overseas Airways comet.

Halfway across the distance to the plane, she felt him tense.

"You can't leave me now," she said. She made it sound like a joke, but she was desperately hoping he wouldn't turn and run.

"I won't," he said.

They reached the ramp and climbed up the steps. At the top, Douglas turned. The small group still waited in the shade, though Julie noticed her father had taken a step forward as though there was one last thing he had wanted to say. She felt the same way, but now she had confidence that there would be time to write and talk and just let the future come for them all.

Douglas stood as though turned to salt. "Douglas..." Julie said.

The stewardess was saying, "You'll have to step in, sir."

Julie thought that she had to be fair. She wanted to drag him into the cabin, but it had to be his own decision. She dropped his hand and stepped into the shadow.

Still he kept looking at the airport terminal, the arcing palm trees, the flashes of bright color and in the distance the island.

"Please, sir..." the stewardess said.

Julie walked back, her heart heavy, toward the seat. She found her seat, avoiding the curious looks of the other passengers. She wouldn't look at the island, she wouldn't look down the aisle.

He wasn't coming. He was staying.

She closed her eyes to fight the tears.

She opened her eyes to see Douglas slipping into the seat beside her. The stewardess was closing the door. The engines of the plane screamed into life.

"I thought you'd changed your mind," she said.

"No," he said. "I just needed to remember how it looks in case I have to think about it later."

He took her hand in his, held her fingers gently and raised them to kiss them.

"We'll come back," she promised him.

He looked at her with the long, dark look.

"Because it's home," she said.

"No," he said, as they felt the plane begin to move away from the terminal. "We'll come back because we want to."

The plane had turned very slowly. They sat silently, holding on to each other's hand. There was a long moment of quiet while the engines drew strength.

Julie and Douglas looked out the small round window at the place where they had been born.

The plane began to move faster and faster, shooting finally from the land and turning to bank for one last glance at the shallows and the beach, the bright green vegetation, the scattered colors of the dwellings. Then it leveled out, heading arrow straight for the horizon of the world where, faintly seen, a new moon glimmered.

* * * * *

About the Author

Stuart Buchan has published extensively in hard cover and paperback. Among his young adult novels are *A Space of His Own* (Scribners, 1979) and *When We Lived with Pete* (Dell, 1986). Born in Singapore, he spent a large part of his childhood in Malaya, the setting for *All Our Yesterdays*. He went to boarding school in Scotland, and later moved to Canada, and then to the United States where he now lives.

Take 4 Crosswinds novels
and a surprise gift
FREE
and preview future books each month.

That's right. When you take advantage of this special offer, you not only get 4 FREE Crosswinds novels and a surprise gift, you also have the chance to preview 4 brand-new titles—delivered right to your door every month *as soon as they are published.* If you decide to keep them, you pay $2.25 each, with *no shipping, handling or additional charges of any kind!*

Crosswinds offers a wide variety of stories about girls and guys you've known, or would like to have as friends, and who share your interests and concerns. And we haven't forgotten romance! Two of our monthly selections are always romances.

As a member of the Crosswinds Book Club, you will receive these four exciting books delivered directly to you. You'll always be among the first to get them, and when you take advantage of this special offer, you can count on not missing a single title!

As an added bonus, you'll also receive our Crosswinds Book Club Newsletter with every shipment. This newsletter gives you the inside scoop on future books and publishes interviews with your favorite authors. It also features a Book Club members Pen Pal Club and prints a special showcase column of reader submissions, queries, comments and letters.

Start with 4 Crosswinds novels and a surprise gift absolutely FREE. They're yours to keep without obligation. You can always return a shipment and cancel at any time.

To get your FREE books and surprise gift, fill out and return the coupon today! *(This offer not available in Canada.)*

·· ═══ CROSSWINDS ᴛ.ᴍ.

ATTRACTIVE, SPACE SAVING BOOK RACK

Display your most prized novels on this handsome and sturdy book rack. The hand-rubbed walnut finish will blend into your library decor with quiet elegance, providing a practical organizer for your favorite hard-or soft-covered books.

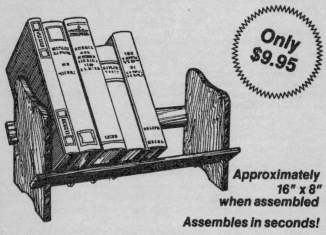

Only $9.95

Approximately 16" x 8" when assembled

Assembles in seconds!

To order, rush your name, address and zip code, along with a check or money order for $10.70* ($9.95 plus 75¢ postage and handling) payable to *Crosswinds*.

Crosswinds
Book Rack Offer
901 Fuhrmann Blvd.
P.O. Box 1396
Buffalo, NY 14269-1396

Offer not available in Canada.

BKR-3R

*New York and Iowa residents add appropriate sales tax.

COMING NEXT MONTH

#961 ENCHANTED—Nora Roberts

The Donovan Legacy

It didn't take beautiful Rowan Murray long to realize that Liam Donovan, her brooding, captivating neighbor, was as mysterious as the lone wolf she'd seen lurking about her cabin. Rowan found herself incredibly drawn to his spellbinding allure—and the secrets that were just beginning to unravel....

#962 THE ADMIRAL'S BRIDE—Suzanne Brockmann

Tall, Dark and Dangerous

Dr. Zoe Lange had admired Admiral Jake Robinson her entire life. Now a dangerous chemical had fallen into the wrong hands, and the only solution was a pretend marriage to her lifelong hero in order to infiltrate their enemy's compound. Would this "innocent" proposition reveal Zoe's *not so innocent* feelings?

#963 EVE'S WEDDING KNIGHT—Kathleen Creighton

The Sisters Waskowitz

Eve Waskowitz was all set to marry the "perfect" man—until he turned out to be a mobster. Unbeknownst to Eve, brooding and sexy FBI agent Jake Redfield had been tracking her infamous fiancé for months. Now he was out to protect *her* from the man she'd almost married, and Eve couldn't be more in love—with Jake!

#964 RIO GRANDE WEDDING—Ruth Wind

Men of the Land

The day Molly Sheffield discovered a wounded man on her land, she knew true love really did exist. One look at the face of Alejandro Sosa and Molly was smitten. But Alejandro needed her help, and his problems weren't that easy to fix. Was Molly willing to put her good name on the line to rescue the man she loved?

#965 VIRGIN WITHOUT A MEMORY—Vickie Taylor

Try To Remember

Mariah Morgan had every reason to fear Eric Randall. He'd kidnapped her and then implicated her in his brother's disappearance. Yet this innocent woman trusted him, and knew he'd find the answers to fill in the gaps in her memory. But once her past was recovered, could she hope for a future with him?

#966 JUST ONE LOOK—Mary McBride

When heiress Sara Campbell got just one look at the face of a serial killer, detective Joe Decker thought his case was finally solved. But Sara had no memory whatsoever of what she'd supposedly seen. Joe was determined to protect his only witness, even if it meant remaining by her side—forever.

In December 1999
three spectacular authors invite you to share the
romance of the season as three special gifts are

Delivered by Christmas

A heartwarming holiday anthology featuring

BLUEBIRD WINTER
by *New York Times* bestselling author
Linda Howard

A baby is about to be born on the side of the road. The single
mother's only hope rests in the strong arms of a dashing doctor....

And two brand-new stories:

THE GIFT OF JOY
by national bestselling author **Joan Hohl**

A bride was not what a Texas-Ranger-turned-rancher was
expecting for the holidays. Will his quest for a home lead to love?

A CHRISTMAS TO TREASURE
by award-winning author **Sandra Steffen**

A daddy is all two children want for Christmas. And the
handsome man upstairs may be just the hero their mommy needs!

*Give yourself the gift of romance in
this special holiday collection!*

Available at your favorite retail outlet.

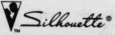

Visit us at www.romance.net   PSDBC

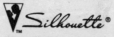

Don't miss Silhouette's newest cross-line promotion,

Four royal sisters find their own Prince Charmings as they embark on separate journeys to find their missing brother, the Crown Prince!

The search begins in October 1999 and continues through February 2000:

On sale October 1999: **A ROYAL BABY ON THE WAY**
by award-winning author **Susan Mallery** (Special Edition)

On sale November 1999: **UNDERCOVER PRINCESS**
by bestselling author **Suzanne Brockmann** (Intimate Moments)

On sale December 1999: **THE PRINCESS'S WHITE KNIGHT**
by popular author **Carla Cassidy** (Romance)

On sale January 2000: **THE PREGNANT PRINCESS**
by rising star **Anne Marie Winston** (Desire)

On sale February 2000: **MAN…MERCENARY…MONARCH**
by top-notch talent **Joan Elliott Pickart** (Special Edition)

ROYALLY WED
Only in—
SILHOUETTE BOOKS

Available at your favorite retail outlet.

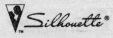

Visit us at www.romance.net

SSERW

If you enjoyed what you just read,
then we've got an offer you can't resist!

Take 2 bestselling love stories FREE!
Plus get a FREE surprise gift!

Clip this page and mail it to Silhouette Reader Service™

IN U.S.A.	**IN CANADA**
3010 Walden Ave.	P.O. Box 609
P.O. Box 1867	Fort Erie, Ontario
Buffalo, N.Y. 14240-1867	L2A 5X3

YES! Please send me 2 free Silhouette Intimate Moments® novels and my free surprise gift. Then send me 6 brand-new novels every month, which I will receive months before they're available in stores. In the U.S.A., bill me at the bargain price of $3.57 plus 25¢ delivery per book and applicable sales tax, if any*. In Canada, bill me at the bargain price of $3.96 plus 25¢ delivery per book and applicable taxes**. That's the complete price and a savings of over 10% off the cover prices—what a great deal! I understand that accepting the 2 free books and gift places me under no obligation ever to buy any books. I can always return a shipment and cancel at any time. Even if I never buy another book from Silhouette, the 2 free books and gift are mine to keep forever. So why not take us up on our invitation. You'll be glad you did!

245 SEN CNFF
345 SEN CNFG

Name	(PLEASE PRINT)	
Address	Apt.#	
City	State/Prov.	Zip/Postal Code

* Terms and prices subject to change without notice. Sales tax applicable in N.Y.
** Canadian residents will be charged applicable provincial taxes and GST.
  All orders subject to approval. Offer limited to one per household.
  ® are registered trademarks of Harlequin Enterprises Limited.

INMOM99   ©1998 Harlequin Enterprises Limited

Darin raised his eyes to her. "Does this mean the baby wants to get out?"

She nodded. "Pretty soon."

Darin grinned at her answer. His exuberant expression took in both his parents. "This is the best birthday ever."

Throat tightening, Cade came between them and slipped an arm around his wife and one around his son, drawing them both closer to him. "You know, I was just thinking the same thing myself."

* * * * *